SHOWDOWN AT DEER CREEK

Other books by D.J. Bishop:

Luke Ludd

SHOWDOWN AT DEER CREEK

•

D.J. Bishop

AVALON BOOKS
NEW YORK

© Copyright 2006 by C.L. Bishop
All rights reserved.
All the characters in this book are fictitious,
and any resemblance to actual persons,
living or dead, is purely coincidental.
Published by Thomas Bouregy & Co., Inc.
160 Madison Avenue, New York, NY 10016

Library of Congress Cataloging-in-Publication Data

Bishop, D. J.
Showdown at Deer Creek / D. J. Bishop.
p. cm.
ISBN 0-8034-9771-7 (alk. paper)
I. Title.

PS3602.I756S47 2006
813'.6—dc22
2005033811

PRINTED IN THE UNITED STATES OF AMERICA
ON ACID-FREE PAPER
BY HADDON CRAFTSMEN, BLOOMSBURG, PENNSYLVANIA

In Memory Of:

My neice: Carolyn D. Smith
who lost her battle with breast cancer at age 34.
1971–2005
"Early detection is the key."

A good, dear friend and neighbor:
William (Jerry) Hudson
1922–2005
A finer man you'll never meet.

A dear and close friend for man years:
Felicia Irene Aldrete
1941–2005
She was the definition of friendship

Acknowledgments

Carolyn Lea

Who, without her love and support
this would be a very sad and lonely world.

Guy G. and Mary Lea Randall

My number one fans and whose faith in my story telling
got me started and kept me going.

L. W. (Jack) and Claudie May (Dollie) Bishop

Two great people who lived it.
A special thanks to Blanche Johnson
Without her friendship and help in editing,
this book would have never been published.

Grateful Appreciation goes to:

Carolyn Lea, Tommie, Virginia, Effie, Mary, Claude, Judy,
Kelly, Jackie, Estelle, Donnie Joe, Joe Lee, Jay, L. W. (Jack),
Claudie May (Dollie), Rocky and Denise
because without their inspiration the story would have never
been told; and a very special thanks to Major Guy G. Randall
U. S. A. F. R.–retired, and his lovely wife Lea for their
undying faith and encouragement.

And Let's Not Forget

All the true cowboys I've had the pleasure of knowing in my life.
May the ones still with us always be mounted and fresh and ride
where the prairie is wide, the air is clean, and the water cool and
clear. And to the many who have already rode over the distant
horizon and faded into the sunset, may they always be remembered
in a good light and where ever they are, may they rest in peace.

Find out more about D. J. Bishop at:
http://www.authordjbishop.com

Chapter One

Four dead in one day, the first to die was Tom Walker. A nicer young man you'd never meet anywhere, and a person the whole town knew, and respected, and Deer Creek's only deputy. Shot down in cold blood, just a month and a half shy of his twenty-second birthday.

Sheriff Lane Tipton had left his long time friend and trusted deputy behind to watch after the jail, the town, and the only other prisoner, a killer by the name of Blackie Getts, while he took another prisoner, Luther Rankin, back to Fort Worth to stand trial for robbery. The sheriff had only been gone two days when the trouble started and by the time it was over the little town of Deer Creek and the lives of all the folks who lived there would be changed forever.

Just an hour or so before sunup on the third morning, four men rode into town from the west, and the last to ride into the glow of the flickering streetlamps was leading an extra horse. They made their way slow and easy along the wide, dirt street all the while looking, maybe even hoping for some sort of resistance from the towns folk, but with the majority of the people still safely in their beds, they got none. Coming to the hitch rail, they drew up in front of the sheriff's office and stepped lazily to the ground. Just moments after entering the jail, the quiet of the early morning was broken by a hail of gunfire. A short time later, they emerged from inside and Blackie Getts was once again a free man.

Before stepping from the boardwalk, Getts paused long enough to survey the little town. He took a long, hard, steady look along the dimly lit street going west, then he let his eyes drift slowly back east, pausing from time to time to make a mental note of each building and what each sign represented. He was not a big man and was not a handsome man, either. In fact, Blackie Getts was down right ugly. He had a full shock of long, black, tangled hair that hung uncombed to his shoulders. And a somewhat, shabby beard of the same color, that grew full and thick on the right side of his face but on the left side, it grew sparse and in places no beard grew at all. Apparently at one time or other, he had been badly injured, and from the looks of things, he had almost been killed. He had one hell of a bad scar, two fingers wide, on the left side of his face just under the eye, and the bottom part of his left ear was missing. No doubt damage left behind from a gunshot that had barely missed its mark, and the scaring had caused his left eye to droop, so bad in fact it never shut completely, not even when he was asleep. He was a short man standing only a tad over five feet, with narrow, sloping shoulders, and skinny arms that seemed too long for a man of his stature. And though his clothes had long ago taken on a ghostly grayish color from the thick layer of trail dust that covered them, at one time they had been dark. Everything, his shirt, vest, pants and hat, had been black at one time. And the awful stomach-turning smell of stale sweat got to where he was going well before he did. He swung his gun belt around his hips and latched it down, then stepped without speaking from the boardwalk.

The men who made up the Getts gang were much of the same stamp as their leader. They were all hard, tough, dangerous men with few cares. All ruthless killers, who would use whatever means deemed necessary to get what they wanted without earning it. Men who had no moral obligation to anyone or anything and would not hesitate to kill man, woman, or child.

R.C. Jacobs had been riding with Getts the longest, a little over five years, and the only person Getts could really count on, and the one person Getts always turned to first to get things done. Standing well over six and a half feet tall, he stood a good head and shoulders above anyone else in the gang; a big, red-faced, raw-boned, square-shouldered man, with powerful arms, and a face that looked to be chiseled from solid stone with a square, rock-hard chin. Long, red hair peeked out from under his old hat brim. And he had the cold, dark, dangerous eyes of a killer, eyes that when angered, would stare deep into the heart and soul of a person just before he pulled the trigger. He had been known to do just that on several occasions. Many a person had lost their lives to the guns of R.C. Jacobs, and several more to the blade of his knife, and he had even beaten one or two men to death with his fists.

R.C. and Getts had hooked-up in St. Louis while both were in jail there for what they considered to be a minor misunderstanding with the law.

Getts had done two years for attempted robbery. He could have gotten several more years, but at the time he committed the crime he was only sixteen, he didn't have a gun, and no one was injured, and as it turned out he didn't even get any money. So the judge gave him two years, with the instructions that upon his release he was to leave the city of St. Louis and the state of Missouri immediately, and for no reason whatsoever should he ever return.

Apparently, he had walked into a hardware store and told the man behind the counter to give him all his money. When the man noticed the smaller and younger Getts didn't have a gun, or knife, or even a club for that matter, he smiled, shook his head from side to side and as he came from behind the counter he said, "no, you're not 'bout to rob me."

Surprised by the man's straightforwardness and readiness to fight, and realizing there was nothing he could really do against the bigger man, Getts mumbled something under his breath the man did not understand then turned and ran out the door.

The sheriff found him early the next morning hiding in an old barn behind an abandoned house on the outskirts of town.

Jacobs, on the other hand, had just turned twenty at the time he had committed his crime three years previous and was sentenced to five years hard labor for almost beating a man to death with a cedar fence post. When Jacobs was questioned, he told the sheriff the man was trying to rob him. But ten days later when the man finally did regain consciousness, he told a much different story. He said Jacobs was trying to steal his horse, and when he confronted him, Jacobs picked up the post and started viciously swinging it.

Upon their release within a month of each other and with no good thoughts in mind for man or beast, they forged the muddy waters of the Mississippi River on stolen horses, in the dead of night, and headed west toward the cattle towns of Kansas. Many a good, hard-working person fell victim to their unbridled brutality along the way. A few survived the torture to somehow live on, but over and over again they'd wished they hadn't. The ones that didn't survive, the ones who were too weak and frail, the ones who were not ready to dig down that deep inside themselves, deep enough to hang onto what little bit of life that remained, turned out to be the lucky ones.

Getts and Jacobs met up with Tatum Stillwell and Hank Hardin late one night in Kansas City, Kansas during an all night porker game in the back room of the Sagebrush Saloon. By the time the sun came up the next morning all four men were dead broke. They had lost every cent to a cowhand from Salina, and neither man was pleased about that, about letting a cowhand beat them at anything. But they knew what had taken them all night to lose; they could easily get back in just a few minutes.

Out on the boardwalk, Getts quietly explained the plan to the others, and moments later he, Hardin, and Jacobs started along the boardwalk in the direction of the hotel.

Hank Hardin was a wide-shouldered, quiet-spoken, stockily built man, with a lightly tanned face that had been aged well beyond his thirty-two years by the wind and sun, and the many sleepless nights he'd spent in the saddle, trying to stay ahead of the law. He had a full shock of thick, wavy, corn-colored hair, which he kept trimmed and combed, and big, round, sky-blue eyes. For most of his life, he had been nothing more than a hard-working cowboy trying to earn a wage. But a little dispute with a mean-spirited cowhand in a cold, overcrowded bunkhouse concerning the last cup of coffee in the pot suddenly changed his life forever. The other cowboy had already had three cups and Hardin knew it. When the other cowboy went to pour the last cup, Hardin called him on it. One thing lead to another and before anyone knew what was going on, lead began to fly. When the smoke cleared the other cowboy was on the floor dead, another had taken an unintentional bullet in the belly and lay dying, and still another innocent cowboy had been shot in the arm. With the law right behind him swinging a hanging noose, Hardin took to the outlaw trails and since that day he had lived as an outlaw. And in doing so he had been forced to live by outlaw rules, which were two simple ones: steal or starve, and kill or be killed.

Showdown at Deer Creek 7

Stillwell watched them go, then turning he walked over and took a seat on the bench in front of the saloon. He was the oldest of the bunch, fifty years old if his count was right, but the deep lines along his sun-darkened face were those of a man much older, maybe by ten years. He was a small man, well under six feet, with narrow shoulders, and small hands. He had a long, narrow, hatchet-shaped face, and a mouth full of rotten, buck teeth, that showed big when he smiled, which he seldom did. He wore a brown suit and tie, and a brown derby hat, that from time to time, a hard gust of wind would blow from his almost bald head, causing him to have to chase it. But the one thing that most made him stand out from the rest was the silver-plated, pearl-handled, short barreled .44 he wore swung low and tied to his leg.

Pushing the derby back, he glanced up the street just as Getts and Jacobs ducked into the alley between the hardware store and the hotel, and he knew then the trap was set. A short time later the batwing doors swung open and out stepped the cowhand. He did not notice Stillwell sitting on the bench as he walked out, nor did he look any direction but straight ahead. At the edge of the boardwalk, the cowhand stopped, then raising his arms high into the air he stretched for a long moment, then after giving his tired, blood-shot eyes an easy rub with both hands, he let out a loud yawn.

Suddenly, Stillwell spoke from the bench. "Been a long night, ain't it?"

The cowhand turned at the unexpected voice, and seeing who it was, he replied. "Yes, sir. That it has been for a fact." But being too sleepy and tired to make small talk, he said, "I think I'll mosey on up the street and see 'bout gettin' a little shut-eye." Throwing up a good-bye hand, he turned and started along the boardwalk toward the hotel. He had not taken many steps in that direction when Stillwell got to his feet and started slowly walking along after him.

The tired cowhand did not pay the funny-looking little man with the brown derby any mind as he made his way along the otherwise empty boardwalk. His mind was somewhere else completely; for the moment he could only think of three things: the hotel just down the street, the clean, soft bed he would soon be crawling into, and after a little nap, a nice hot bath and shave. It wasn't until he saw the man hunkered down behind the water trough at the entrance of the alleyway and realized it was Hank Hardin, another man from the poker game, that the little man walking behind him took on any real meaning, but by then it was too late.

The outlaw suddenly sprang from behind the water trough with his pistol drawn, at the same instant the cowhand felt a hard blow to the back of his head, and the next thing he knew, someone had grabbed his gun, and another had clamped a hand over his mouth and he was being dragged kicking into the alley. He felt a hand grab his hair from behind and yank his head backward, and the last thing he saw in life was the cold, killing eyes of R.C. Jacobs as he plunged the blade of his knife deep into his belly.

That was four years ago, and for the last three of those years they had been down Mexico way running

Showdown at Deer Creek 9

along the border, crossing over into Texas from time to time to rob a stagecoach, or bank, or to rustle a few head of cattle. And it was going well until Getts made the mistake of thinking they could rob the bank in Presidio. As they rode into town someone recognized them as possibly being men on the run and notified the sheriff. And when Blackie and his gang came out of the bank they walked straight into an onslaught of gunfire.

All but Getts managed to somehow get away, but just before riding clear, his horse was shot out from under him, and when Getts hit the ground, his head was leading the way, and the hard blow knocked him out.

A week later, in the early morning hours, R.C. Jacobs led the men back into Presidio. And when they rode out again they had Getts and some other man from the next cell named Bull Ansel with them. The new comer was tall and lanky and he had no neck to speak of, his head just seemed to grow from his shoulders, but while in jail Getts had taken a liking to him and decided to take him along. The sheriff and his two deputies lay in a pool of blood on the floor.

Now they were in the little town of Deer Creek doing the same thing.

With his newfound freedom, Getts wasted no time in ordering a search of the town for the two men who had seen him shoot the drifter that night in the Double Deuce Saloon. It was only by their account of the shooting that Getts had landed in jail on a charge of murder, awaiting the circuit judge.

Apparently the drifter had seen Getts slip a card from the bottom of the deck. And when he called him on it, Getts drew a belly-gun and shot him in the face. The drifter was dead before he hit the floor.

Getts and his gang of killers made their way slowly across the street in the direction of the Double Deuce where Getts knew he would find the first witness.

Red, the bartender, had been sweeping the floor in the storeroom when he heard the gunshots coming from the jail, and had just started in behind the bar to take up his shotgun when the batwing doors suddenly flew open. He looked up as the men entered, and when he realized the last man to walk through was Getts, he quickened his pace, but before he could reach his shotgun lying under the bar, all five men had shot him at least once. And with Red lying behind the bar in an ever-growing pool of blood, Getts stood over him with a big, wide, smile and fanned another five more shots into his already bullet-riddled body.

"Now," Getts said, in a loud, cold voice. "I don't reckon you'll be stickin' your nose where it don't belong anymore, will you?" Turning to his men, he slowly holstered the still smoking Colt, and added, "one down and one to go." Cutting a quick eye to R.C., he said, "take the men, leave no stone unturned. I want that other loudmouth found, and found today, and when you do find 'im I want 'im in the same shape as this one here and that smart-talking deputy over there in the jail is in." Getts paused, and after taking a long, careful look around the saloon, he said, "R.C., on second thought, just take Hank with you. While you two are doing that I want Bull and Tatum to round up every person in town and bring 'em here. We'll just take over this little town." He reached up and gave his beard an easy rub. "Yes, sir," he said with a sneer. "We'll just make ourselves right at home while we wait on that Mr. Do-Good sheriff to get back from Fort Worth. I've got a little something to settle with him before we light out of here." He added dryly, "no man puts Blackie Getts in jail and lives to tell about it. No man."

"Why wait on the sheriff to get back, Blackie?" R.C. asked. "I think we should clean out the bank and light a shuck."

"How many times have I told you, R.C., don't think, that's my job. Leave the thinking to me and just do your job, and that is to do what I tell you to do, when I tell you to do it." Getts glanced in the direction of Bull Ansel and Hank Hardin standing by the door then back to R.C., "that is unless you're thinking 'bout maybe trying to take over my job. And if that's what you've got in mind you better fill your hand, but let me tell you something right now, and I think you already know it, R.C., you're not nearly fast enough to get the job done."

"Oh, Blackie," R.C. replied, while moving his hand well clear of his pistol. "There's no need for all of that. I just thought the time we're going to spend waiting on that sheriff, we could use putting some miles between us and this town, and you know if that posse from Presidio ain't give up and turned back they can't be far behind us. That's all I was talking about."

Getts slowly shook his head and said, "R.C., are you tellin' me you're afraid of a few lawmen? We've had lawmen after us before."

"No, that's not what I'm sayin' at all. Just forget I

said anything. Just forget it, Blackie. I can't talk to you when you're like this. Can't nobody talk to you when you're like this." Turning, he jerked his head toward the door and said, "come on, Hank."

When the men were gone, Getts walked behind the bar, and after giving the bottles sitting on the shelf a look, he reached and took one. Taking it up to his mouth, he grabbed the cork in his teeth and gave it a twist, and at the same instant a pull and the bottle opened with a loud pop. He reached up to take the cork from his mouth, but suddenly stopped, and after a moment of what seemed to be serious thinking, he spat the cork at the bartender's dead body. Reaching under the shelf, he took a clean glass, then turning, he made his way slowly back around the bar, and as he walked, he mumbled, "what do I owe you for this fine bottle of whiskey, Mr. Loudmouth?" Then as if the dead man had spoken, Getts spun back. "What's that? You'll have to speak up, I didn't quite hear what you said. Oh, it's free? Why thank you, Mr. Loudmouth, thank you very much. And if I'm ever back in this neck of the woods I'll be sure to stop in again."

Turning, he made his way to a little table by the window facing the street. Then hooking the toe of his boot around one of the chair legs, he slid it back and dropped down, and sat for a moment just staring out the window at the empty boardwalk. Then as he lifted the bottle slowly to his mouth, he said in a low voice, "this is my town now." He turned the bottle up and drank down four big gulps, then after wiping his mouth with his sleeve, he slowly filled the glass, and sat the half empty bottle down on the table. "Why," he asked himself, in a low voice, "why in the world does R.C. let me do it? Let me talk to him any such way? I just don't know. Any other man would be dead before he got the second word out of his mouth."

Getts knew R.C. Jacobs to be as bad as they come with a knife or gun, rifle or pistol, it made no difference. He was a dead shot with both, and with either hand, and maybe even a little faster on the draw than Blackie was. And he was no slouch when it came to his fist either. Over the five years they had been riding together Getts had never known of R.C. ever backing down from anything or anybody and the word fear was just nowhere in his way of thinking, but yet he just sat there and let Getts talk to him the way he did.

Getts drew his gun, flipped open the cylinder, and gave it a spin. And as he watched the six spent cartridges roll by, he said under his breath, "he knew I was out of bullets, too." Turning the pistol up, he shook the spent cartridges out, and slowly, one by one, reloaded it. With that done, he shoved the pistol back deep into the holster and slipped the leather thong over the hammer.

He had just poured the third glass of whiskey when the sudden sound of many shuffling feet coming along the boardwalk got his attention, and a second later, the batwing doors flew open and Getts looked up to see Bull and Tatum, bringing in the first of the townsfolk.

"Now what have we here," Getts asked, while pushing up from the table, "some more do-gooders no doubt."

Leading the way was a tall, older man wearing a nice suit and tie who stood right at six feet, with a full head of neatly combed, silver-gray hair. "Now see here," he said, but before he could say anything else, the barrel of Getts' gun came down against the top of his head and stopped him. There was a short painful groan and blood immediately spewed from the hole in the man's head, his eyes rolled back, and his knees buckled, sending him helplessly to the floor.

"My God," the woman standing closest to the man screamed. "Please, oh God, please stop, you're going to kill him." She dropped to the floor beside the injured man. Tears ran freely down her narrow, aged face as she cried, and pleaded for mercy. Then thinking of what needed to be done, she opened her handbag and took out a handkerchief and placing it over the wound, she quickly applied pressure hoping to stop the bleeding. Suddenly, she looked up at Getts through red, tearstained eyes and cried out, "you killed him. Oh, my God, you've killed my husband." She swallowed hard, and gave the tears running down her face a quick swipe with her free hand and when she looked back at Getts she added in a hard but somewhat calm voice, "you're a murderer, sir, and a coward."

Grabbing her by the arm, Getts jerked her abruptly to her feet. "He ain't dead, but he's going to be, and you too if you don't shut your mouth." Pushing her roughly toward the back of the saloon, he added, "now get back there and shut up. Not another peep out of anybody." He gave a half-hearted laugh. "All you good folks of Deer Creek can just relax. Yes sir-re-bob, you sure can

Showdown at Deer Creek

'cause I ain't going to hit anyone else. No, I sure ain't, but if you don't do as I say, I'm going to shoot you. I'm going to shoot every last one of you graveyard dead." He paused, looking at the man on the floor. "Now some of you good towns folk drag this old piece of buzzard bait back yonder out the door, and no talking, and if I was you, I wouldn't go trying anything foolish, you hear?" He turned, and started back to the table by the window, but as he started to sit down, he looked out to see R.C. and Hank coming along the boardwalk on the far side of the street. They had their guns drawn, and three men were walking out front with their hands held high in the air.

One was a small man, not too tall, very thin, with a long, narrow face, and hooknose, wearing a white apron.

The second man was bigger, much taller, well over six feet, with thick, wide shoulders, powerful arms, and big hands, and he also wore a long apron but it was black and made of leather.

The third man was somewhere in between. Not too big and not too small, and for sure no one who would stand out in a crowd, but he looked somewhat like the man Blackie had sent his men to look for, the other loudmouth.

In anticipation of getting rid of the second witness so soon, a faint smile came to the killer's lips. But after a closer look and realizing none of the men was the one he so desperately wanted to kill, the smile quickly vanished, and with it went what little dab of patience the killer possessed. His face instantly grew dark with anger as he stormed toward the street. Getting to the batwing doors, he pushed them open with so much force they almost broke from their hinges. Once out on the boardwalk, Getts suddenly stopped, drew his gun, and without saying a single word to anyone, shot the smallest of the three men twice in the stomach, right dead center of his clean, white apron.

The little man grabbed at the sudden pain with both hands, his face went blank, and his mouth twisted. He staggered back trying to distance himself from the growing pain, but it was not to be.

"Lamar." The bigger man called out, while extending a helping hand to the falling man, but with life gone he could not be helped, and with one last hard gasp for air, the man slid slowly to the ground and lay dead.

The bigger man spun on his heels, his eyes red with hatred, but his face white and stiff with fear. Looking up, his eyes locked on Getts standing on the boardwalk. "What are you people doing?" he shouted. Then motioning to the dead man, he said, "this man has never done harm to you or anyone else. If he was guilty of anything it was for being too nice. That's Lamar Tuggle, he was no threat to you or your kind, he was no gunfighter, he ran the hardware store." He paused, then shaking his head in disbelief, he added in a mild voice. "He'd go out of his way to lend a helping hand to anyone, he would give a man his last penny." He took a long, fast, defiant step toward the boardwalk, and as he did, he screamed out, "and now you've shot him dead for no reason."

Showdown at Deer Creek   17

Getts quickly thumbed the hammer back on his pistol. "You take another step, mister, and I'll blow your fool head off. Now if you think I'm bluffing, you're just one step away from finding out."

The man, knowing he was hearing the words of a just proven cold blooded killer, came to a sudden stop and raised his hands.

Getts let out a big, loud, belly laugh, and when the laughter had faded, he looked over at R.C., motioned with the gun barrel toward the dead man, and said, "since Mr. Tuggle there was such a good-hearted and helping person that would give a man his last cent, I don't reckon he'd mind one little bit if you went through his pockets." Glancing at the bigger man, he said, "what I want from you is the name of the other man, the man who did all the talking to the sheriff. We've already taken care of that big, fat, loudmouth bartender in there. I want to know the other man's name and where I can find 'im."

"I don't know who you're talking about," the big man answered abruptly. "And if I did," he said with a hard, defiant shake of his head, "I for sure wouldn't tell the likes of you."

Getts eyes narrowed, and he raised his gun with the intentions of shooting the man, but as he tightened his finger on the trigger, the third man called out, "it's Mushy Crabtree. That's who you're looking for. He works out at the Running T for the Townsends. They've got a cattle spread eight miles west of town."

The big man turned quickly to the man talking.

"Watch your mouth, McNare. Just shut up and don't say anymore."

Getts leapt from the boardwalk and raced toward the big man. "No, you're the one that's going to shut up, and you're going to shut up right now." When Getts got within reach, he swung the gun at the man's head, but the big man ducked and received only a glancing blow to his left shoulder, but still with enough force to cause him to lose his balance and he fell, landing flat on his back in the street. He instantly pushed at the ground, struggling to get back to his feet, but the killer stood over him with his gun drawn. "You get up from there," Getts shouted, "and I guarantee you, you're a dead man."

The big man figured he was about to die but then realizing there was no real point in getting himself killed this early in the game stopped his attempt to stand and just relaxed back on his elbow.

"Now there," Getts said with a grin, "ain't that better? You're gettin' yourself all worked up over a bunch of nothing." Then turning to the third man, he said. "Now, sir, what were you saying just before this fellow so rudely interrupted you? First, why don't you tell me your name?"

The man looked down at the big man. "We might as well tell 'im, Sam. They're going to kill us all if we don't." Cutting an eye back to Getts, he said in a low voice. "The name's McNare—Evret McNare. I run the livery stable across the way. And that there," he said pointing to the big man, "is Sam Stovall. He owns the leather goods store."

Getts looked down. "Well, I'll be, you're a saddle

maker huh? I want you to take good care of yourself Mr. Saddle Maker. I sure do 'cause I might need me a new saddle before I leave here." Glancing back to McNare, he said, "the other man. I want to know 'bout the other man. This Mushy or whatever it is you called 'im."

"Mushy Crabtree, that's his name. He works for big Bear Townsend out at the Running T. He comes into town ever week or so to pick up supplies for the ranch. That's why he was in town the night you killed that feller."

Instantly, Getts left hand came up catching McNare solidly across the nose and mouth with the back of his hand. "I didn't kill anybody!" he shouted. "It was self-defense. He drew on me first, it was either him or me, and the whole town knows it."

The force of the blow drove McNare's head sharply back, causing him to stagger backwards several steps, but he somehow managed to get his feet back under him and came to a staggering stop. He stared at Getts with a hard eye, while wiping at the trickle of blood running from the corner of his mouth with the back of his hand and as he did, he said, "how could he have drawn on you first, Getts? No one found a gun on 'im or near his body."

"Why, you're a little loudmouth, too." Getts said. Then jerking his gun up, he fanned two quick shots into McNare's chest. The little man never knew what hit him and a second later his life, too, was gone.

Getts turned back to Sam Stovall, lying on the ground. "Now, you got anything to say? If you do, just go ahead and get it said so I can kill you, too."

Sam looked up into the cold, dark, murdering eyes of Blackie Getts, and knew if he said anything, anything whatsoever, Getts would kill him. He knew too, that he must somehow stay alive; he had to stay alive so he could figure out a way to get word to the sheriff, or to the men out at the Running T if he or any of the rest of the towns folk expected to get out of this thing alive. He knew too that Getts had started out wanting to kill just two men because they had seen him kill the drifter and had told the sheriff what they saw. But now the whole town had seen him kill four innocent men. That meant every person in Deer Creek was now a witness against Getts and his gang of murderers.

"Get up." Getts said to Sam Stovall. Then motioning toward the saloon with his gun barrel, he added, "get in there with the rest of your do-gooder friends." Then looking over, he said, "Hank, get Bull and Tatum, and move these two, poor, dead souls out of the street here, put 'em over there in the livery stable, cover 'em with hay or something to get 'em out of sight. Oh yeah, y'all need to move that bartender out of the saloon, too, we for sure don't want him to start stinking. Then I want you two to go round up the rest of the fine towns folk, those do-gooders." Turning, Getts hitched his pants and led the way up the steps through the batwing doors.

As Sam entered, R.C. gave him a hard shove from behind, pushing him well toward the back of the saloon. "Get back there with the rest of 'em, and don't open your mouth until someone tells you to."

Getts dropped into the chair at the little table, and R.C. took a seat across from him. "What are we going

Showdown at Deer Creek 21

to do with all of 'em?" Jacobs asked, leaning across the table. "Hell, Blackie, every last one saw you shoot those men."

Getts started to answer, but his words were cut short by the sound of a youngster crying. Jumping up from the table, he quickly made his way toward the back of the saloon, where he found the source of the unwanted noise. A woman sat with two small children. A little black-haired boy of about seven years, and a little red-haired girl, maybe a year or two younger. It was the little girl doing the crying. "Shut her up." Getts shouted.

The woman nervously pulled the little girl closer. "I can't shut her up," she said in a broken voice. "Can't you see she's scared?"

Sam, trying to take the attention away from the woman and children spoke up. "Getts, that's Mrs. Mahony. She's owns the Longhorn Café across the way, and those are her children, Josh and Mary."

Getts looked in Stovall's direction, then quickly back to the woman. "Café huh?"

The woman nodded and answered. "Yes, sir."

Getts smiled. "In that case, I want you to go fix me and my men something to eat, and be quick about it. I'm hungry." Looking to the woman still holding the handkerchief to the gash in her husband's head, he added, "and you can take that old windbag over there with you. But y'all watch what you do, because if you mess up, and believe me I'll be watching, I'll shoot you both, and then I'll shoot these two kids here."

The women got to their feet, then picking up the two small children, headed for the batwing doors.

"No, sir." Getts said as he stepped to block their path. "No you don't. You leave the kids here," then added in a loud voice, "what do you take me for, a fool? You two just go fix up some grub. The saddle maker here can watch after those whining brats, and he better keep 'em quiet."

After the two women had left, Getts walked behind the bar and got another glass. Then, back at the table, he filled the glass and pushed it slowly across to R.C. Then in a low voice, he answered R.C.'s earlier question. "What do you think we're going to do with 'em, R.C.? We're going to kill 'em, and then we're going to torch the town."

"Kill all of 'em?" R.C. asked.

"Yes, sir," Blackie answered with a hard nod, "every last one of 'em and then we're going to burn the town down. Nobody locks Blackie Getts up and lives to tell 'bout it . . . nobody."

Chapter Two

Charles Townsend sat quietly behind the large oak desk in his study working on the ranch books. It was the very same desk his father had sat behind as the president of the Northeast Bank of Boston for better than twenty-five years. He was a big, tall man, with wide, thick shoulders, powerful arms, and big, hard, callused hands. And unlike his father who was already badly balding at his age, he still had a full head of silver-gray hair that he kept neatly trimmed and combed and long, thick sideburns of the same silver-gray color. And it was because of Charles Townsend's bigger than average size that most folks called him Bear, a name his father had given him when he was barely knee-high to a short horse and a name that had stayed with him throughout his life. He was not a fancy-dressed man by any means, though he had enough wealth that he could dress anyway he wanted. It just so happened he preferred his work jeans, and shirt and the same old tanned leather vest he'd been wearing for years. From time to time he would, however, put on one of his nice tailored suits and tie, but that didn't happen often. And only then after much pleading from the two people who meant more to him than life itself, his beautiful daughter, Rebecca, and the only living of his two sons, Zachary. His oldest son, Robert, had been killed in one of the last big Indian raids over six years back. And just a short two years before he got killed, Anna Townsend, their mother, and family matriarch, was suddenly stricken with an unknown illness, and in spite of all Bear, or anyone else could do, passed away due to a bad fever. The event almost destroyed Bear, but realizing that with their mother gone the kids needed him more than ever, he pushed the pain he felt way down deep inside, and since that day he had lived one day at a time, but every day for his children.

As a young man he had attended schools in Boston and in Philadelphia where he studied banking and finished at the top of his class. He was an honest, hard-working man who had fought tooth and nail for every inch of the Running T. And over the years he had developed a good eye for cattle and land and he had enormous respect and admiration for the men around him. For he knew if not for them, there would not be a Running T or for that matter anything else. Men like Boots Morgan, Porter Dobbs, and Mushy Crabtree, all good, honest, hard-working men and the very first three cowboys to ever ride for the Running T brand. If not for those three, the house would not have been built, or the barns and the corrals for that matter, and the first Indian raiders would have never been turned back.

Out of the three, only one was alive: Mushy Crabtree. Boots Morgan drowned crossing the Brazos back in '69 during an awful rain-storm. And Porter Dobbs was found just east of the down turn of Cottonwood Creek with a half-dozen Kiowa arrows in his body.

Bear Townsend was grateful to those men and to all the others who had stood beside him over the years and given their all against sometimes losing odds, men who put their lives on the line each day for nothing more than a month's wage, and the sake of riding for the brand. And he was a fair and descent man, and one who would never ask another man to do anything he himself could not or would not do.

The first twelve years after coming to this land were the most trying. It seemed like the men at the Running T were always fighting someone. If not the Comanches, or the Apaches, it was the Kiowa. And if the Indians weren't enough, they also had the outlaws coming through just one step ahead of the law, most riding the trail south to Mexico. And there were the rustlers, the ever-present rustlers, men wanting to get something for nothing, something someone else had worked hard for, and over the years there had been no shortage of those caliber of men. Bear did not respect the rustlers and showed hostility and hatred toward them when they were captured.

"Daddy—Daddy, come quick." A loud, excited voice called out. Then, Bear heard the all too familiar jingle of spurs and footsteps on the porch, and a split second later, the front door opened with a bang as it swung back hard against the wall.

He looked up from his work to see his pride and joy running into his study. "What are you trying to do, girl, tear the house down?" But seeing the excitement in her beautiful green eyes, he quickly pushed up from his desk and as he stood, he asked, "what in the world's wrong, Becky?"

"Oh, Daddy, come quick. It's Bell; she's having her colt."

A big smile came to the old man's face as he stepped around the desk to meet her. Then taking his daughter by the hand, he led the way to the front door where he suddenly stopped. Reaching over, he took his gun belt from the peg and swung it around his hips and latched it in place. Then grabbing his hat, he slapped it on as he walked out onto the porch. Their spurs jingled in harmony as they made their way down the steps, and Bear had to quicken his gait to keep up with his daughter who was almost dragging him toward the barn.

Rebecca Townsend was an attractive young woman, tall and slender, with big, beautiful, green eyes and long, red hair that hung almost to her waist in huge curls. And like her brother and father, she had clothes for any occasion, but for the most part she preferred jeans, a long-sleeved shirt, her old black, flat-crown hat and boots. But her prized possession were the big rowel spurs she had won several years back in a shooting match with a drifting cowboy who thought he was a fair shot, he wasn't as good as Rebecca. No matter how she was dressed on any given day, her uncommon beauty and poise always seemed to make the heads of both men and women turn when she'd pass by. Most days she dressed simply because she worked like everyone else on the Running T, that is from the back of a horse. The back of a horse was no place for anything fancy, and for sure it was no place for a dress.

As they approached the huge double doors of the barn, a man emerged wearing a narrow-brimmed, Texas style hat, a dark-blue flannel shirt and an old, beat up pair of chaps. His face was clean-shaven, leaving only the thick, silver-gray, dropping mustache that covered his top lip. When Becky saw him, a big smile came to her lips. He was a much smaller man than her Pa, and stood a good three inches short of six feet, but to Becky, Mushy Crabtree was a giant among men. And although he was no real kin, he had always been known as Uncle Mushy to her and both her brothers, and it was a title he seemed to be very proud of.

"Just coming to get you, Bear," the man said, while worriedly shaking his head. "We've got trouble, big trouble. I don't think Bell's going to be able to have that colt on her own." He paused to think then added, "I sure do hope it's not so, but I'm a-thinking it's bridged and if it is we'll have to get its head and legs turned back straight so she can have it."

"Bridged," Rebecca echoed. Quickly looking over at her father she asked, "Pa, what are we going to do?"

"We'll just have to give the old gal some help," Bear

answered, but seeing the unsure look on the face of his ranch foreman, and longtime friend as he spoke the words, he asked, "what is it, Mushy? Why in the world are you looking so worried? This ain't the first colt we've had trouble with and I'm sure it won't be the last."

"You just said it, Bear. Bell's getting up in years. That mare has got to be, what, fourteen, maybe fifteen years old?"

"She's fifteen, Uncle Mushy." Rebecca quickly answered. "Pa gave her to me on my twelfth birthday and she was three then."

The sudden memory brought a smile to big Bear Townsend's lips; he had picked the steel-dust filly from the herd that spring knowing Rebecca was quickly coming of age and would soon be needing a good horse. That Fall, he and Mushy took their time in gentling the horse, making sure there was no more spook left in her, and that she had no bad habits. Then he remembered, just like it was only yesterday, the day that he, her mother, and two brothers had given Rebecca the horse. It was her twelfth birthday. They had finished their midday meal and were sitting on the front porch eating cake when Mushy lead the horse, wearing a new saddle with a big red bow tied to the pommel, from the barn. When Rebecca realized what was happening, she sprang to her feet then leaping from the porch, she ran screaming with joy toward the horse. Moments later, her oldest brother, Robert helped her up into the saddle and that was the last anyone saw of her until supper. And from that day to this day the only time the two had ever really been apart was when Rebecca went back east to live with her Aunt Effie for three years while she attended finishing school. Of course, for the last few years Rebecca had not been riding Bell as much as she once did, but she did, however, ride one of Bell's nine sons everyday, all of which Rebecca had gentled herself.

Suddenly a loud, pain-filled squeal coming from inside the barn brought Bear back from his pleasant thoughts and put his mind back on the present situation. Looking west, he stared in the direction of the setting sun. Its bright, orange glow streaked dark by thin, wispy clouds was quickly fading as it settled upon the distant horizon. Its golden, finger-like rays fighting for life lay upon the many cottonwood and pecan trees surrounding the house, and also the barns sending their shadows long and jagged across the land. "It'll be dark soon," he finally said while turning to Mushy. "You better light the lanterns. We may be in for a long night." Then turning, Bear led the way into the barn and down the long hallway to Bell's stall. For the moment, the old horse lay on her side atop a thick layer of hay, but sensing the presence of Rebecca, she slowly raised her head, and rolled her eyes in the direction of the gate and when she saw her longtime companion, she nickered a low heartfelt greeting, but being too weak and tired to hold her head up for any length of time she let it drop back to the hay.

"Oh, Bell." Rebecca said, as she dropped to her

knees beside her old friend. Then gently stroking the horse's face and all along her neck, she said in a low, loving voice, "it's going to be alright, girl, Pa and Uncle Mushy are here."

At that instant, Bear felt a warm flush wash over him and a big lump caught in his throat. He wanted to speak, but the words would not come out. For that one brief moment, he thought he'd seen a tear well up in Rebecca's eyes, something he or no one else had seen since her brother Robert had died, and just one other time before that, when her mother passed away. Tears did not come easily for Rebecca Townsend, and for her to even come that close, Bear knew her heart had to be breaking. He moved closer and placed his hand on her trembling shoulder and as he did he said, "we'll do the best we can, Rebecca. But as much as we'd like it to be, sometimes your best ain't always good enough."

The girl looked up at her daddy through red, tearstained eyes, and as she did, she gave his hand a little squeeze and said, "I know you'll do your best, Pa. And I know one day Bell will leave us and there won't be anything anyone can do to save her. I'm just not ready for it to be today."

Bear gave his daughter a light, understanding pat on the shoulder and was just about to say how lucky Bell was to belong to someone like her when he was interrupted by the familiar sound of Carmen, the old Mexican housekeeper ringing the dinner bell. Knowing the horse didn't need to be left alone, Mushy stayed to watch after her while Bear and Becky went to the house to eat supper. And while they ate, Carmen, who was

Showdown at Deer Creek

also the wife of Campo, the ranch cook, gathered blankets from a bedroom closet and had them stacked neatly in the rawhide chair by the door. Full of food and coffee and with only the flickering glow of the lantern lighting their way, Bear and Becky picked up the blankets and, after saying good night to Carmen, headed back to the barn.

"Mushy," Bear started, "you go on to the cook shack and get a bite to eat and some shut-eye; we'll watch after this deal here."

"I've done had supper, Bear. Campo brought me a plate a bit ago. And I was thinking 'bout maybe just beddin' down out here somewhere," he answered, then throwing up a hand toward the next stall, he added, "maybe in there on that soft pile of hay. I don't know just when things are going to start happening, but I'd say if Bell's going to have that colt, she'll have it before first light."

Bear gave a grateful nod and said, "ok, if you're sure that's what you want to do. We'll be more than happy to have your company and your help, too, when it comes time."

With that decided Bear and Mushy spread out their blankets and crawled in to get some sleep, but Becky had thrown her blanket over the old horse and sat softly petting and talking to her in a low voice.

Bear reached up to pull his hat down to block the lanterns' bright glare. And it was then he noticed not the little girl he had raised sitting there, but the beautiful young woman she had grown into, the young woman who in less than two months would be married.

His heart ached at the thought, and his mind instantly jumped back the fifteen or so years to the first time he ever saw his soon to be son-in-law.

It was getting along to late Fall, a sudden cold snap had dropped the temperature and the cold, icy, north wind was howling. Bear and the men had just returned from two weeks of checking cattle on the north range. That night over supper, his lovely wife Anna told him that three days back she and Carmen were hanging wash on the line when they noticed a boy walking along by himself. Not knowing who he was or what he was up to, they did not approach the young man, but did watch through a window as he snuck into the barn. He had not been seen or heard from since. She did, however, say she had taken a couple of blankets, and one of Bear's old coats along with a plate of hot stew and a big glass of buttermilk and sat them just inside the barn door and when she went back the next day with more food, the blankets and coat were gone and the plate and glass were empty. Not only were they empty, but they had been washed clean.

"What in the world is a boy doing way out here all alone?" Bear asked.

"I don't have any idea," Anna answered. "But we didn't see another soul anywhere, no wagon, no horse, nothing, just him."

"Why didn't one of the men say something to him?" Bear asked.

"I sent Robert to the bunkhouse with word that if

they did happen to see 'im not to pay 'im any mind," Anna answered, then added, "I knew you would know what to do when you got home." After a short pause, she said, "Bear, he's all by himself, he's cold, and hungry, and probably scared, and he's not much more than a boy. I doubt if he's more than a year or maybe two older than Robert over there."

Bear glanced at his oldest son, then at the other two children sitting at the table, and as he turned his attention back to his wife, a smile came to his lips. "Well," he said as he slowly pushed up from the table, "I guess I better go have a talk with the young man."

"I want to go," all three kids echoed at the same time.

"No, ya'll stay here in the house with your mother." At the door Bear buckled on his six-gun, slipped into his coat and grabbed his hat, then turning, he looked back at his family and said, "I'll not be long." Out on the porch he stopped, and looking west he saw light shining through the windows of the bunkhouse that told him the men were still getting about, and just a few yards to the north, he could see movement in the cook shack, probably just old Campo cleaning the pots and pans after supper. But looking toward the barn, Bear saw no light and the only sound being made was an occasional snort from the horses that mingled in the corral. Suddenly, a brisk north wind stirred, causing Bear to grab at his hat with both hands and the sudden coldness made his eyes water. Pulling his coat tight, he stepped from the porch and started in the direction of the barn knowing there would be no light until he lit one of the lanterns hanging on the peg just inside the door. But if that boy, as Anna so tenderly calls him, is up to no good and in the right place when I open the door, I might not ever get a chance to reach for the lantern, he thought to himself as he walked toward the barn. For he knew, and knew all too well, just because the boy was young didn't mean he could not or would not do harm. As a matter of fact, that's how Pappy Wheeler had lost his life. Pappy had hesitated for no more than a blink of an eye when he saw the Kiowa boy coming from behind the tree and that's all the time the boy needed to send the spear flying that struck the old man in the chest. And Bear remembered Pappy Wheeler's last words as he lay dying in a pool of blood: *Bear, he's just a little boy.*

Bear slowly opened the barn door and eased through. Reaching up with his left hand, he took a lantern from the peg and with his right he struck a match. As the flame grew on the wick, the inside of the barn slowly emerged from the darkness and shadows danced without direction along the walls, and from the rafters high above an old barn owl hooted his dissatisfaction at the sudden bright light and took wing.

Bear started to move deeper into the barn, but when he did his foot struck something. He glanced down to see it was nothing more than a plate and glass setting by the wall, both empty, and both freshly washed. "I know you're in here," he called out in a loud, hard voice. Then reaching down, he drew his pistol and slowly thumbed the hammer back. "If you're in here," he said while letting his eyes search the outer reaches of the flickering lantern, "you better show yourself." He stood for a long moment, listening, looking, but heard or saw nothing. Then moving one foot at a time, he worked his way along the wall of the barn and as he did, he gave each stall a good, careful look.

Suddenly, a low voice coming from above broke the silence with the words, "I don't want any trouble, mister."

"Well now, that kinda gives us something in common then, don't it," Bear answered. "'Cause I don't want any trouble either, but I do want to know who's been staying in my barn, eatin' my grub, and drinkin' my buttermilk."

"I didn't steal it," the voice answered back. "Some lady brought it and put it by the door. Nobody came to fetch it so I ate it."

"I'm glad you did," Bear said. "'Cause it would have surely went bad just sittin' there. Say why don't you come on down and let's get to know each other. My name is Charles Townsend, but my friends call me Bear, and might I ask what your name is?"

There was a long pause then the voice said, "Lane. My name is Lane, Lane Tipton."

"Well now, that's a mighty handsome name. I like that name, I sure do. Say, Mr. Lane Tipton, do you live around these parts or are you just passin' through on your way to somewhere else?"

"I don't reckon I live anywhere now, and there ain't nowhere else."

"Where's your Ma, and Pa?"

"Dead," the boy answered, then added, "the Injuns got 'em over a week ago, got my sister, too. They're all dead."

"I'm sorry to hear that, son," Bear replied in a low,

shaky voice, but once the sudden shock of the boy's statement had subsided Bear said, "why don't you come down and we'll go up to the bunkhouse where it's a mite warmer."

For a long moment there was no talking and no movement, then Bear heard a light rustle, and looking up, he saw a sprinkling of hay drop from the loft as the boy started to move. At the ladder the boy hesitated, but after a bit he started down, taking one rung at a time. The first thing Bear noticed was the boy had no shoes or hat and the sleeves on the old coat Anna had given him were a good foot longer than his arms.

"That's a mighty fine coat you have there," Bear said. "But it looks to me like it's a mite big."

"Yes, sir, it is, but it's warm," the boy answered. And as he turned from the ladder, Bear Townsend got his first look at the little skinny, dark-haired boy who had lost his family to the Indians. His face and hands were covered thick with dirt and his clothes were ragged and worn, but the part that stuck out more than any was the unforgettable sadness in his big brown eyes. Then Bear noticed the large, red welts on the boy's face, and his right ear was swollen to almost twice the normal size. "What in the world caused all those red marks there on your face." Bear questioned.

"Scorpions," the boy answered. "I got 'em when I hid from the Injuns under that old, big, cottonwood deadfall. When they'd sting it would hurt like all-get-out, but I couldn't make any noise and I couldn't even slap at 'em to get 'em off of me 'cause the Injuns were standing all around, so I just had to bite my lip and take it." The boy then raised his shirt, and showed Bear even more bites on his belly and back.

Bear's body shook as he imagined the agonizing pain the boy must have gone through. Then taking the boy by the hand, Bear led him up to the bunkhouse, and while Campo put some Dr. Blacks Ointment on the scorpion bites, Bear introduced him to Mushy and the men and after finding the boy an empty bunk, it was not long before he was in it and sound asleep.

Before the week was out, Anna had moved Lane out of the bunkhouse into one of the spare bedrooms in the house. And from that day on all four children, Zachary, Robert, Lane, and Becky had been raised as brothers and sister. But all of that somehow changed while Becky was back east in finishing school. When she returned home, there seemed to be a different sparkle in her eyes when she and Lane were around one another. And it was not long after Lane got elected sheriff of Deer Creek two years ago and moved from the ranch into town that their intentions were made very clear. It happened one Sunday evening when Lane came courting. So it didn't come as a total surprise to Bear or anyone else for that matter when six months back, Lane had asked for Rebecca's hand in marriage. Now they were getting married in less than two months; in two short months his little girl would be gone.

Suddenly, the quietness of the night was broken by several loud, painful grunts from Bell that instantly brought Mushy and Becky to their feet and Bear's eyes popped open.

"It's time," Mushy called out.

"I must have dozed off," Bear replied, while getting groggily to his feet.

"I say you did," Becky answered with a laugh, "the way you were snoring, Pa, it's a wonder the roof of the barn didn't cave in."

Mushy quickly moved in behind the horse so he would be in position in case she needed help. "Becky," he called out, "you get there by her head and see if you can keep her calm, but watch out for those front feet of hers, she's going to start thrashing 'em 'bout."

"Ok, Uncle Mushy."

"Bear, you get in here beside me. It might take the both of us to yank this one out, but we don't want to bother her until she needs us to."

For the better part of an hour, the old horse would push, then relax. Push then relax. Finally, she took a deep breath, then straining with every fiber in her body she gave a push.

"Here it comes," Mushy called out. "That's it old gal. If you can give me one more push like that one maybe it'll be over." And just like the old horse had understood what the man was asking her to do, she took another deep breath and with even more force than the first she gave a push.

"There's the head," Bear said.

"Just one more push." But before Mushy could get the words out of his mouth, the horse pushed and the colt came out. Mushy quickly wiped the colt's nose to clear it, then taking a straw he stuck it in one nostril and gave it a wiggle then the other, and the response was what he expected, a sneeze, and the breath that followed brought life to the small, wet, helpless body.

Bell, knowing what needed to be done next, rolled just enough to get her feet under her, then standing, she started cleaning her new son. Within the hour, the baby had stood and walking on wobbly legs, found a tit. As he suckled, his tail swished back and forth like a leaf in a high wind.

"You did good, girl," Becky said giving Bell an easy pat on the neck. Then turning to her Pa, she smiled and added, "ten colts and not a filly in the bunch and all steel-dust, too."

"That there has sure been a fine mare," Mushy cut in. "But I think we should make this her last one."

"I believe you might be right," Bear replied. "I think it's time to say she's done enough. Well, anyway we've done all we can here. I think I'll mosey on up to the house and try to get a little sleep. Y'all might want to think about maybe doing the same."

"I think I'll stay out here for a while, Pa," Becky answered.

"No need in me going to the bunkhouse now," Mushy cut in. "It'll be light in a couple of hours, time to go to work, but I think I will ease on over to the cook shack here in a bit and see if Campo has a pot of coffee made up."

Bear threw up a good-bye hand as he headed for the door. Becky took up a hand full of dry hay and started drying the colt. Mushy took care of the livestock at the barn, and left, headed in the direction of the cook shack, mumbling to himself something about needing some coffee. Again all was quiet and with the new colt now bedded down in the corner of the stall, Becky shook out her blanket and lay down. She lay for a good, long while just staring up at the rafters of the old barn, remembering the countless hours she and her brothers had spent swinging from those rafters and all the plans they had made together while playing among the hay in the loft. And it was in that loft her Pa first found Lane Tipton, the boy who had since then grown up on the ranch and was now the love of her life and the man she would soon marry.

The thought of her upcoming wedding day brought a smile to her beautiful lips but then a lonely sigh, for she had not seen Lane in over a week and knew it would still be at least another week if not longer before he got back from Fort Worth. "But what if something bad has happened to him?" she thought out loud to herself. "Surely nothing has or Tom Walker would have ridden out to let us know or he would have at least sent someone with word." The next thought caused her eyes to widen and she sprang to her feet.

"Mrs. Mahony," she said out loud, "today is the day I was supposed to go in and let Mrs. Mahony fit me for my dress." *I need to get about,* she thought. *I need a bath and I need to pack a bag with clothes, enough for three or maybe four days.* Before leaving the barn, she gave Bell grain and after toting water and filling the trough, Becky checked on the colt, then picking up the blanket she started toward the house.

This was Rebecca's favorite time of the day and it

always had been. The air was cool and damp and to the east the sun was just starting its climb for the heavens. At the chicken pen a rooster crowed and moments later another. At the corral, dust rose high as the men were catching their horses, and high in the cottonwood near the house a nightingale called out loud to its mate. But first I need a cup of coffee, she thought to herself. *A good hot cup of coffee would taste mighty fine 'bout now.*

Bear sat at the dinner table sipping a cup of coffee and knew who it was when he heard the door open and by the time she entered the room he had already poured a cup and had it sitting at her place on the table.

"Thought you might be ready for some coffee," he said as she entered.

"You were thinking right, Pa," she replied as she dropped into the chair. Picking up the cup she gave it a short cooling blow then took a taste. "I just remembered, Pa. Today's the day I need to go in and let Mrs. Mahony fit me for my dress. The material came in over two weeks ago."

Bear looked over and said, "I remember you saying something 'bout that here a while back. But why is it, Becky, you're letting Mrs. Mahony make the dress and not Mrs. McNare? She's the one with the dress shop."

"I know Pa, but Mrs. Mahony will do a good job and she needs the money. She's got them two kids and she's just barely gettin' by down at the café. It's been awful hard on her since Ray died. Mrs. McNare has always done well in the dress shop, and Evret has the livery stable. Anyway, I've talked to Mrs. McNare and she understands and she did make a little money by selling me the cloth. So I'll get Mrs. Mahony to make the dress, that way I'll be helping them both out some."

Bear smiled at his daughter's way of thinking and said, "I'll get Mushy or one of the men to drive you in."

"No need. I'll drive myself. I'm going to stay in town a day or two. I've got so much to do and so little time, and you can tell Uncle Mushy that I'll pick up the supplies and bring them back home." She took a sip then looking over the rim of the cup through the rising steam she asked, "have you got a list ready?"

He gave his head an easy nod and answered, "yes, ma'am, I sure do. It's right over there on the cupboard. But I need to check with Mushy first, 'cause I think Campo's got a few things to add to it."

"While you're doing that, Pa, I'm going to take a bath and change clothes." Then calling out she said, "Carmen, if you would please, ma'am heat a little bath water."

"*Bien, señorita* Becky, I will."

Bear pointed with a hand, "if you're hungry, there's bacon and bread over yonder on the stove that Carmen cooked up."

After breaking a biscuit, Becky added bacon and dropped back to the chair. Then looking across at her father she asked, "what's wrong, Daddy? You seem to have something on your mind."

Bear took a deep, ragged breath and gave his head a worried shake. "You're right, Becky. There is something on my mind. It's you and all this marryin' stuff and leaving home. Are you sure 'bout this? Are you sure Lane is the man you want to spend the rest of your life with? If you're not, then now's the time to speak up."

"Oh, yes, Daddy, I'm sure. I've never been so sure of anything in all my life. And you know as well as I do that Lane is a good, honest, hard-working man. You should know 'cause you and Uncle Mushy are the ones who taught him."

"I know he is, but I just don't know if he's good enough for my daughter."

"But in your eyes, no man will ever be good enough, and that's the way it's supposed to be. But Pa, I'm happy and I want you to be happy for me, too."

"Oh, I am. I don't know what I get to thinking sometimes, Becky. Oh, yes, I do. I get to thinking about this big old house without you in it. Zack is always out with the men, and Lane's moved to town, and with your mother and Robert both gone that's kinda going to leave me by myself. Of course there's Mushy, he ain't goin' nowhere. And Carmen will still be here, and I guess she will be until something happens to her. God, I hope nothing does or I won't be able to find anything around here."

Becky stepped around the table and took a seat on her pa's knee. She put her arms around his neck and as she did, she leaned down and gave him a little kiss on the forehead and at the same instant a big tight hug and said, "I love you Bear Townsend and no matter where I'm at or what I'm doing I will always be your little girl and you will always be my daddy." Then standing she added, "but if I don't get about, I won't get to town before dark."

"You go get ready," Bear said while slowly getting to his feet, "I'll tell the men to hitch a team."

A short time later, Becky walked out of the house with a bag in her hand. Looking west she saw her Uncle Mushy coming with the buckboard and her pa walking toward the house from the barn. "How's she doing?" Becky asked as her pa approached.

"Just fine," he answered. "It look's to me like you might have your hands full with that one, Becky. He's in there right now gettin' ready for you; he's bucking, and kicking up a storm." Then stopping he asked, "you sure you don't want someone to drive you in?"

"Pa, really, there's no need in sending anyone with me. I've been up that trail at least a thousand times. I'll be ok. And if someone did go they'd just have to turn around and come back."

Mushy reached over and took the bag from her, and after placing it in the back, he took Becky's hand and helped her up into the seat, a ritual Becky really didn't care for. On several occasions over the years she had fussed with her Uncle Mushy about it, but Mushy, thinking it only proper for a man to help a lady into a seat, did it anyway. Then with a smile and an easy flip of the lines the team started and she was on her way.

Bear stood alongside his longtime friend and watched her go. And once she was out of sight, he turned and said, "I don't know what I'm going to do without her around."

"Oh, she'll still be around," Mushy replied, "just not as much. You ain't going to get rid of her that easy. It probably won't be long before you have three or four

Showdown at Deer Creek 45

little nappy-headed grandkids running wild all over this place."

Bear looked at his old friend and smiled. "You know she'd been hard-pressed to have found a better man than Lane."

Mushy gave a nod. "I agree with you all the way; he's a good one that's for sure." Then giving Bear a friendly slap on the back he said, "let's go in and see if we can maybe find us a cup of coffee. Is there any left?"

"Have you ever been in my house when there wasn't any coffee?" Bear asked as he led the way up the steps.

"I've seen times not only was there none in the house but there wasn't any on the whole place."

"Yeah, but that was only because the Indians had us penned down and couldn't nobody get to town."

The buckboard moved easy along the sometimes rough but constantly dusty trail. The only sounds were the clomping hooves against the hard ground and the steady jingle of the trace chains. From high in the light-blue, cloudless sky the sun shined bright, and its golden rays lay hot upon the land. From time to time a light, cool breeze would stir from the west giving Becky a welcome break from the heat and suffocating dust.

At Tub's Crossing, Becky drew up to let the horses drink, and when they'd had all they wanted she tied them off to a nearby tree. Then walking to where a large, flat rock stuck out some distance in the stream, she dropped to her belly and drank of the cool, sweet water, and when she'd had her fill, she took off her bandana, wet it, and wiped the trail dust from her face and neck. But knowing she had no time to linger, she made her way across to the buckboard untied the team and after climbing back into the seat she started the team along the trail toward Deer Creek. If she was going to get to her destination before dark, she knew she needed to be moving along.

Some hours later and just as the sun was beginning to settle on the western horizon, the buckboard topped the rise just west of town. In anticipation of seeing Mrs. Mahony and the kids and with hunger pains stabbing at her insides, Becky flipped the lines and the team quickened their gait. Moments later, she drove past the little schoolhouse at the edge of town and when she noticed it had a new coat of brown paint, she smiled. It wasn't until she started along the street that she noticed something wasn't right. The street was empty, not a man, woman, or child could be seen anywhere, and there were no horses standing tied at any of the hitch rails. Not even the old spotted dog that hung around the livery stable had greeted her as he normally did. All of a sudden a great wave of fear washed over her; her heart raced and her pulse quickened. Realizing danger lay ahead, she drew hard on the left line trying to turn the team around, but just as they started to turn a man ran from the alley yelling and waving his hat causing the horses to come to a rearing stop. Becky instinctively reached down for her six-gun, but as she brought it up, another man leapt on the side of the buckboard. Reaching across he grabbed the pistol from her hand, and before he stepped back to the ground he took her Winchester from beside the seat.

"Now Bull, who do you reckon we have here?" the big, tall, red-faced man asked.

"I don't rightly know, R.C. You tell me. But whoever she is, she's awful easy on the eyes, ain't she?"

R.C. Jacobs walked around and extended his hand. "Here, ma'am, let me help you down."

"You'd be better served to give me back my guns," Becky replied. Then looking toward the man holding the horses she said, "and you, sir. If you know what's good for you, you'll let loose of that team immediately and let me be on my way."

R.C. gave a laugh. Then grabbing Becky by the arm he jerked her from the buckboard and slammed her hard to the ground. "I don't know who you think you are," he said looking down, "but when I tell you to do something—"

"Hold up, R.C.," a loud voice called out from up the street, "that's no way to treat a guest."

Becky looked in the direction of the voice to see a short, dirty man with a shabby beard and a badly scarred face coming along the boardwalk. By the time the man had reached the buckboard, Becky had gotten to her feet.

"Bull, you take the wagon and team and put 'em away." Then looking at Becky he asked, "for what do we owe the honor of your visit to my little town?"

"Your town?" Becky questioned. "This ain't your town, and if it was, I for sure wouldn't be here."

Blackie Getts eyes instantly shot fire, and as he stormed toward Becky he drew his gun, but for some reason stopped short of coming down on her head with it. He studied the girl for a long silent moment then said, "you came close, you came awful close Little Missy. But if I was you I'd watch my mouth, 'cause I won't put up with no sort of smart talk."

"Hey," R.C. cut in, "it says here on this rifle plate: "To Rebecca Townsend, happy sixteenth birthday love daddy."

"Townsend," Blackie echoed. Then glancing back at Becky he asked, "your daddy's the one that's got the big spread west of here?"

"Yes, he is and if I don't get back, he'll come looking for me and he'll have men with him."

"Let me have her," a loud distant voice called out.

Becky looked up to see a much cleaner, older man walking toward them at a fast pace wearing a suit and brown derby hat.

"Stillwell," Blackie replied, "are you out of your mind? I'm not going to give this girl to you or anyone else, and she ain't for sale either."

"Name your price, Blackie. I'll give you all I have in my pockets plus my part of what we take from the bank, what do you say, how 'bout it?"

"No!"

"How 'bout if I throw in my saddle? You know you've always wanted that saddle of mine and now would be a good time for you to get it."

"I never really wanted that junky old saddle. If I'd wanted it I would have just shot you and took it. If you want a woman that bad, Tatum, you can have that old windbag or that woman with those two whining kids or any of the rest of them old hags in there, just take your pick, and it won't cost you a dime. But you can't have this one."

"No, I want her, Blackie."

"You can't have her, and if you try anything, Stillwell, if you lay as much as a finger on her, I swear, I'll kill you." Then turning to R.C., Blackie motioned up the street and said, "put 'er in there with the rest of 'em and keep a close eye on her, R.C. This one here is full of fight."

"Let me go this instant," Becky shouted. Then looking Blackie Getts straight in the eye she said, "my father will see you dead for this." But as she spoke the words she had her doubts because she had told her pa she would be staying in town for three maybe four days. So she knew unless he or one of the men just happened to ride in for some reason, nobody would come looking until the fifth day. She knew too, it would be at least that long if not longer before Lane got back from Fort Worth. Then she noticed the old man with the derby hat kept staring at her and she wondered how long Blackie Getts would be willing to reject his offer. But if she could just find Tom Walker or Sam Stovall maybe one of them could tell her what these men wanted, but more importantly, maybe they could tell her where the rest of the townsfolk were.

Chapter Three

Two men rode tired and hungry through the dim light of the evening. Both weary from a long day in the saddle, still they rode on, but only one seemed to be anxious to reach their destination and he rode out front leading the horse the man behind was riding. He was a tall, lean man with a muscled frame that stretched well over six feet, with wide, square shoulders and chest that tapered down to a small waist. He wore a black flannel shirt and dark jeans that were covered mostly by a pair of batwing chaps and shading his head from the hot sun was a fairly new black, flat-crowned hat. He made his way slow and easy along the trail staying to the brush and riding well below the skyline, his dark, brown eyes always on the move, looking, searching the trail ahead both near and far for signs of a pending ambush or anything that might cause him to lose his prisoner or his life.

"Sheriff, ain't we ever going to make camp?" the one riding behind asked, then added, "in case you ain't noticed it's near dark."

Sheriff Lane Tipton reined in his horse, then looking back at the other man he said, "I was hoping to make camp on up the trail somewhere about Ponders Creek."

"Ponders Creek," the man echoed quite loudly, then shaking his head in disbelief he said, "that's still another three hours or better away. I'm 'bout to starve, ain't you gettin' hungry?"

"Rankin," he said, "I won't ever get you to Fort Worth if we keep stopping."

"You just can't wait can you, Sheriff? You just can't wait to get me back to Forth Worth, can you?"

"It's not so much getting you back to Fort Worth that's brothering me Rankin," the sheriff answered. "The fact is I need to get back to Deer Creek. I have a town to look after." But as Lane spoke the words he knew Deer Creek was not the real reason for his riding so hard. He knew too, he had left a good man watching over the town and Tom Walker could handle most anything that might arise, and if not, he had Sam Stovall to give him a hand if he found himself in need of help. No, it was not so much the town Lane needed to get back to; the real reason for his wanting to get back was so he could be with Becky Townsend, the woman he loved and the woman he would soon marry.

There was a long silence then Luther Rankin said, "I wish you'd call me Tater; that's what people have called me all my life. And Sheriff, while I'm talking

I'm going to say it again. I think you know as well as I do that I didn't do what they say I did."

Lane cut a hard, quick eye at him. "I don't know anything of the kind, Rankin. Anyway, saying whether you did or didn't ain't my job, that's the judge's job. My job is to see you get back to Fort Worth to stand trial. Just remember, I didn't come lookin' for you. I got a poster saying you were wanted for robbery, and if you hadn't come riding into Deer Creek the way you did I wouldn't have seen you, but since I did, I had to arrest you. Heck, I've got nothing against you. The fact is I kinda like you, Rankin, but if I don't take you back, then I'm not doing my job, and the way I see it that's what's wrong today; there's too many people around not doing their job."

"Doing your job," Rankin half shouted. "You doing your job is going to get me put in jail, for no tellin' how long, for something I didn't do. Worst yet it might even get me hanged." He paused to think, then added, "yes, I was in Fort Worth, and yes I was in the Silver Dollar Saloon. But no, I was not in the alley, and no, I did not hit anyone over the head with a butt of a gun, and no, I did not rob anybody."

"They say they've got an eyewitness, a man who saw you rob the man with his own two eyes."

"If someone said they saw me in the alley that night they're either badly mistaken or they're a damn liar, 'cause I wasn't there."

Lane took off his hat and wiped at the sweatband with his handkerchief, then before slapping it back on, he roughly ran his fingers through the thick, damp, black hair trying to shake off some of the sweat. Then standing tall in the stirrups, he let his eyes search along the tree line for a place to make camp, for he too was hungry and tired, and even though there was still daylight left he was sure a good hot cup of coffee would perk him up. He rubbed at his mustache with an easy hand while studying the lay of the land, then he threw up a pointing hand and said, "over yonder in that stand of cottonwood." Touching his horse forward, he rode from the trail headed in the direction of the little grove of trees.

After taking care of the horses, Lane gathered wood from a nearby dead-fall and started a fire. Then filling the coffee pot with water from the canteen, he sat it over the flames.

"You need some help," Rankin asked. "I'd be more than happy to give you a hand with doing that."

"No, I'll manage," Lane answered. Then after taking time to think he said, "if I was you, I wouldn't go trying anything, Rankin. If you do, I'll shoot you."

"I'm not trying anything, Sheriff. I just asked if I could help, that's all."

"Well, I'm just saying that better be all you've got on your mind."

Cutting the top from a can of beans, Lane poured them into a pan to heat, then he sliced bacon into a skillet and as it started to fry he looked across the fire in the direction of Luther Rankin who sat cross-legged on the ground, his hands still handcuffed together. He sat with his head hung low and his eyes cast toward the ground. He was an average built man with dark, collar-length hair and small brown eyes that for some reason always seemed to smile. His shoulders were narrow, and his legs slightly bowed, obviously the product of many miles in a saddle. From day one he had not acted as though he had anything to hide, and when Lane and Tom Walker arrested him that night in the Double Deuce Saloon, he had not put up any fight whatsoever and from that day he had maintained his innocence. And the story he told was the same each time. But apparently there was a witness, a person who saw him rob the man in the alley. On the other hand, Lane had known of witnesses being wrong. Could it be Luther Rankin was innocent of the crime of which he was charged? Maybe the eye witness had made an honest mistake, maybe the witness had been drinking, or was too far away to get a good look, or maybe it was like Rankin had stated and for some unknown reason the man was lying. "I don't know," Lane mumbled to himself, then giving his head a worried, unknowing shake he gazed into the flickering flames of the campfire and thought, I just don't think this man has it in his heart to be a thief.

When the bacon had fried, Lane dipped food to a plate and with it in one hand and a hot cup of coffee in the other he started in the direction of his prisoner, but as he approached he realized Rankin had fallen asleep. "Here," Lane called out, then giving the man an easy nudge with the toe of his boot, Rankin opened his eyes.

"Here," Lane said. "It's time to eat. It ain't much but it's all I've got."

Rankin gave a thankful nod and took what was offered, but as Lane turned to walk off, he asked, "I don't reckon you'd even consider taking these cuffs off while I eat," but before Lane could respond Rankin said, "I guess not. You wouldn't be doing your job."

For a long moment, Lane stood without speaking, just looking down at the man sitting there, then reaching into his shirt pocket, he took out the key. "Ok," he said. "I'm going to take 'em off but just until you eat. And let this be fair warning, Rankin, if you try anything, anything at all, I'll shoot you dead and take you the rest of the way to Fort Worth draped over your saddle."

"You don't have to worry, Sheriff, I'm not going to try anything."

"Oh, I'm not all that worried, Rankin," Lane answered, "but you better heed my warning 'cause you won't get another."

Back at the fire, Lane took up his own plate and started to eat, but he did so with one eye on his plate and the other on Rankin.

A light breeze stirred among the branches high in the tall cottonwood and the leaves hummed to the rhythm. To the north a pack of coyotes cried in harmony to the rising moon, and to the west a lone nightingale called out for its mate.

"We better turn in," Lane said while getting to his feet. "Daylight will be here before you know it." After rolling out their bedrolls, Lane put the handcuffs back on Rankin and with that done they both lay down, but sleep did not come easy for Lane because every time he closed his eyes, somewhere in the back of his mind a picture of his beautiful Becky would appear. In some of the images, she danced on a hillside covered thick with bluebonnets, her long, white dress and red hair flowed to her movements. And in others she was just sitting in the swing on the front porch smiling, but no matter what the image she was always beautiful and always smiling. And this night was no different than all the others because Becky Townsend was the last thought in Lane's mind when he finally did somehow manage to doze off.

Some hours later, and for no apparent reason, Lane's eyes opened wide in the darkness. For a long moment he lay perfectly still, trying to figure out what it was that had so abruptly awakened him. Slowly, and without moving his head, he let his eyes roll in their sockets in the direction of the fire to find it had died out, then to where Rankin was still bedded down, then to the horses. They stood with their heads high, their ears perked, and their nostrils flared, and he knew then someone or something was close by. Then he heard something that made his blood chill; voices. Someone was talking and not far away. Quickly, he grabbed his six-gun from its holster, then getting to his feet, he moved slowly and hunkered down to where Rankin lay. Dropping down to one knee, he clamped his hand over Rankin's mouth and when his eyes opened, Lane took his finger up to his lips for quiet. "There's someone out there," he whispered. "I don't know who or how many. All I know is I heard voices."

Rankin looked up, his eyes full of surprise, then extending his hands he said in a quiet voice, "Sheriff, take 'em off, and give me my gun."

"Just hold on," Lane answered. "I'll go have a look. You just stay where you're at, and if I was you I wouldn't even think about running."

"Sheriff, you gotta take these handcuffs off," Rankin pleaded, "you can't just let someone walk in here and shoot me dead."

Lane shook his head no, then turning he walked from camp, his outline quickly fading into the night. He moved slow and easy through the darkness and tangled brush, moving one foot then the other. Coming to a little clearing he drew up beside a large cottonwood and stood for a long moment trying to hear the voices again but after hearing nothing, he moved on. Topping a little rise, he walked off into a dry creek bed and as he broke over the top on the far side his mind told him to stop. Again he stood perfectly still, straining with every fiber to see, but in the darkness sight was not there. Then came the faint sound, the sound, he was now sure, of people whispering to each other and they did not appear to be more than ten yards away. He dropped down to all fours and started to crawl, and before long he was in position to make out what they were saying.

"It's got to be here somewhere," the first voice said.

"John, maybe what you saw wasn't a campfire at all," the second voice answered, a woman's voice.

"Mama, I'm hungry," a third voice interrupted.

"I know you are baby and maybe it won't be long before we can all have something to eat."

"It's all my fault," the man's voice cut in. "If not for me and my big ideas, y'all wouldn't be out here in this godforsaken place, we'd still be in Pine Bluffs where there was at least food to eat and water to drink."

"It's nobody's fault, John," the woman said. "We both agreed to come here and start a new life, and talking like that ain't doing nobody any good."

"Those dirty varmints," the man said. "If I ever get my hands on those three sorry devils I'll kill 'em—I'll kill 'em all. I swear I'll kill 'em, Kate."

"You're not going to kill anyone, John. You're too fine a man for that, and anyways, we won't ever see those men again. They're gone and the wagon and all our belongings are gone too, and we may die before we find help."

"Don't talk like that, Kate. We're not dead yet and with God's help we're not going to die. Now I know I saw a campfire and all we've got to do is find it before daylight or whoever it was that built it will be gone, too."

"John," the woman started, "what happens if we do find the fire and its more outlaws? What are we going to do then?"

There was a long, silent pause then the man said, "surely my luck ain't that bad. But if it is maybe they'll go ahead and shoot us. That would be less painful and quicker than us walking around out here starving to death."

Lane had heard enough to know that no more than

Showdown at Deer Creek 59

twenty feet away a family, or at least a man, woman, and child were searching the darkness for his camp, and someone had taken their wagon and left them to die. But not knowing for sure if they had a gun, he didn't want to make any sudden moves that would startle anybody and cause them to shoot into the night. Thinking, he ran his hand along the ground until he found a rock. Picking it up, he tossed it to where if they did shoot at the sound it would be away from him.

"What was that?" the woman asked.

"I don't know," the man answered, "but it came from over that way."

"It's the law," Lane called out. "I'm the sheriff of Deer Creek. You folks hold your fire and I'll come to you." Then he heard the woman say in a low peaceful voice, "thank you, Lord."

When he got to where they stood huddled, Lane instructed them to hold hands and he would lead them to camp and a short time later they broke from the brush. But it wasn't until after Lane stoked the fire and got it going, that he got his first good look and what he saw was something he would not soon forget.

They were dirty and their faces badly drawn and their clothes showed signs of blood where sharp rocks, sticks, and the thorns of the mesquite had taken their toll.

The man was short, with narrow, slopping shoulders, and skinny arms, and a thick black beard covered his face.

The woman on the other hand was heavier built with a rounded face and body and big, beautiful dark eyes. She had a pleasant little smile that from time to time would appear, but Lane could see the worry and fear in the woman's eyes and knew she was probably only smiling to keep from crying.

But what caught Lane's eye the most was the little girl with the long, corn-colored hair wearing the blue dress. She would not look up at him and had not spoken a word even when he had spoken to her.

"Have you got any water?" the man asked. "We haven't had anything to drink for two days and the same for food."

Reaching over, Lane took up one of the canteens and handed it to him.

Quickly pulling the cork, the man let the little girl drink first then the woman, and when they had had their fill, he turned it up himself.

"I'll have some coffee ready here in a bit," Lane announced. Then moving the skillet over the flames, he sliced bacon into it and added beans to the pan. "Don't have any bread," Lane said, "but we've got beans and bacon."

Rankin sat quietly on his bedroll and when the lady noticed him, he smiled, tipped his hat and said, "Evenin' ma'am."

She nodded back but stared long and hard at the handcuffs.

"You folks want to tell me what happened," Lane asked.

"Three men rode from the brush with their guns at the ready." The man answered. "They ordered us down from the wagon and after they searched us for anything we might have in our pockets, two of 'em crawled up to the seat and drove off toward the west, and no sooner than they were out of sight we started walking east." The man took a sip of water then added. "Everything we had is in that wagon. It ain't right, them just taking it that way and leaving us out here in the middle of nowhere to die." He turned an eye to Lane and said, "that was two days ago and now we're here."

"If you don't mind me asking, where are you folks from?" Lane asked.

"We're from Arkansas," the man answered proudly, "a little town called Pine Bluffs. It sets right square-dab on the west bank of the Arkansas River about fifty miles south of Little Rock."

"Our name is Olsen," the woman cut in.

The man quickly turned his eyes in the direction of his wife, then looking back at Lane he said, "oh my word, where's my manners?" Putting out his hand he said, "my name is John Olsen and this is my wife, Kate and our daughter Olivia. She's named after her grandmother on her mother's side."

Lane took the man's hand. "Glad to meet you, Mr. Olsen," he said, then tipping his hat to the lady he added, "you too, ma'am. My name is Lane Tipton and that gentleman over there," he said, pointing, "is Luther Rankin."

"It's Tater," Rankin replied. "Everyone calls me Tater."

Kate Olsen gave a nod and said, "glad to meet you, Mr. Tater."

Suddenly at a time when there was not much to smile about, the camp came alive with laughter, even the little girl, who had until now not made a sound, managed a heartwarming giggle at the name Tater.

When the food had cooked, Lane filled two plates and using the skillet for the third the newcomers started to eat. But as they did Lane could not keep from thinking about what he was going to do with these three. He couldn't just ride off and leave them here. For they had no food or water and he knew the nearest town was Ponders Creek. He also knew he needed to get Rankin on to Forth Worth, but on the other side of the coin, he couldn't just let the three men who had taken the Olsens' wagon get so far ahead their trail would fade away. Then realizing there was but one thing he could do, he said, "we'll take you folks on to Ponders Creek in the morning. There you'll have plenty of water and before we leave we'll see 'bout killing some meat. I've got a few cans of beans there in my saddlebags. That should be enough to hold you until we get back with your wagon."

"You're going after those men?" John questioned.

"Yes, sir, we sure are," Lane answered. "Just as soon as we get you folks settled somewhere where you'll be safe and I'm a-thinking Ponders Creek is just the place."

John Olsen instantly turned and grabbed his wife, giving her a hug of joy, then turning back to Lane he said, "Sheriff, you'll never know how much me and the wife appreciate this."

"It'll be my pleasure," Lane replied. Then looking over to the little girl he added, "we just can't have men running loose that'll do something like this." Walking over to the fire, he added wood and as the flames grew he stared deep into their yellowish-red glow. He stood for a long moment without speaking, then suddenly turning he said, "we'd better see if we can maybe get some rest."

"Here, Mrs. Olsen," Rankin said getting to his feet, "you and the little girl there can have my bedroll. I'll just move over here by this tree."

"Oh, no, we couldn't, Mr. Tater. But I do thank you for the offer."

"You might as well, 'cause I ain't going to use it. I've already had so much sleep my joints are startin' to stiffen."

"Well, if you're sure then," Kate said, "but we're not looking to put anybody out. You've already done enough, and you've saved our lives."

"What will put me out is if you and the little one don't lay down there and try to get some rest." Then leaning back against the trunk of one of the cottonwood trees, Rankin closed his eyes.

"Go ahead and take mine," Lane said talking to John. "I'm going to sit here at the fire for a bit and drink this cup of coffee."

"Thank you, Sheriff," John said, then giving a thankful nod, he repeated the words, "thank you."

It was not long before the camp grew quiet and all but one was asleep. Lane sat at the fire watching the flames dance along the newly placed log, while sipping at the coffee. He was using the time to think about how anybody could be so hard-hearted to just leave a family to die. He knew this hard, unforgiving land was not short on men of that caliber, and he knew, too, with the passing of each day the number was getting smaller. If he could find the men who had done this to the Olsens, there would be three less the world would have to deal with.

At first light, Lane added coffee to the pot and moved it over the flames and while it brewed, he saddled the horses. Back at the fire, he dropped cross-legged to the ground beside Rankin who sat sipping coffee from one of only two cups in camp. John and Kate Olsen were sharing the other and the little girl sat quietly in her mother's lap with her head down scratching at the ground with a stick.

"We're going to have to take it slow," Lane finally said. Then looking over at John, he added, "Mr. Olsen, since the little girl's not very big I think that bay will carry all three of you if we go slow. Me and Rankin will double up on my horse, but if I see it's going to hurt 'em then someone is going to have to walk."

"I understand," John replied with a nod.

"Here," Rankin cut in, "you want some coffee?"

Lane took the cup and after taking a sip he said, "Mr. Olsen, can you tell me what those fellers looked like. What were they wearing and such?"

"You bet I can," was the answer. "The one that seemed to be the leader was a big man well over six feet tall and not weighing an ounce under two hundred and fifty pounds. His hair and beard were long, thick and black. And even in this terribly hot weather he was wearing a heavy buffalo skin coat and an old beat up hat that should have been done away with long ago, and he was packing what looked to be a .50 caliber Sharps rifle."

"He smelt like a buffalo, too," Kate interrupted.

John gave his wife a quick glance and an agreeing nod, then looking back at Lane, he continued. "The other two looked a whole lot like brothers to me. Both were skinny with long, tangled black hair, and thick, full beards. And both were wearing buckskin shirts and pants and they, too, had big bore rifles." He paused to think then added, "you can't miss 'em, and for sure you can't miss that wagon of mine. It's got a brand new white canvas top and four of the finest Arkansas mules you've ever laid eyes on pulling it. And if 'n they ain't killed and eat 'em, there's an old brown and white spotted milk cow, and a fine zebra-striped dun horse tied to the back."

"Once we get you folks settled," Lane said, "I'll go see if I can find 'em."

"They ain't gone far," John replied, then giving his head a knowing shake he added, " 'cause that wagon of mine is loaded a mite heavy, and as good as they are those mules can't pull it no more than five miles a day, seven at best. 'Course we might have got more out of 'em if we'd been running from the law."

Lane stood and after kicking dirt on the fire, he loaded the coffee pot and cups into his saddlebags. And with that done he helped Mrs. Olsen up behind her husband, then picking up the little girl, he placed her in the saddle in front of her pa. Walking to his horse, he swung up, then kicking a boot free of the stirrup so Rankin could get his foot in, he reached down and took Rankin's hand, pulling him up behind him. Just as the sun started to peak above the oak to the east, Lane put an easy spur to the horse and moved out slowly in the direction of Ponders Creek.

A good bit short of midday, they drew within sight of the creek and none too soon because under the added weight the horses were starting to tire. But while easing along looking for a place to make camp a white-tailed doe jumped from the brush and had almost got out of range when Lane pulled the trigger on his Winchester. Now they had meat. Lane wasted no time in stripping the saddles, then after the horses had drank, he led them to a little knoll just west of camp where the grass grew tall, thick and green. There he put the hobbles on and made his way back to camp. "We'll let 'em rest a while," he said. Then drawing his knife he began making the deer ready to cook. Later while washing his hands at the creek, he reached up and rubbed at the week's growth of black stubble on his face and thought of the razor in his saddlebags, but with so much to do he decided against a shave, knowing he had to find the Olsens' wagon. Depending on what happened when he did find it would determine if he would have three more men to take to Forth Worth or three dead bodies. But for him to get back to Deer Creek he knew these things had to be done and the sooner he got started the sooner he would get back to where he was really needing to be.

After the meat had cooked, they ate and when they

had finished, Lane saddled the horses. "Here," Lane said to Mr. Olsen. He slid the Winchester over to him. "I want you to keep this rifle. We might not get back for three maybe four days, and you may need to do some huntin'. I've got my handgun and I've got Rankin's pistol there in the saddlebag if I need it."

"Much obliged," John answered with a nod. Then putting out his hand to Lane, he added, "I want to thank you, Sheriff, and we'll be right here when you get back."

After helping Rankin into the saddle, Lane stepped up himself, then spinning the horse he threw up a hand as they rode off. For a short time Lane thought seriously about riding northwest in hopes of finding the deep ruts left by the heavily-loaded wagon, but instead he lead the way due west knowing if he could find the trail left by the Olsens, he could back track it to spot where the robbery had taken place. By the time they arrived back to where they had made camp the night before it was getting late and the sun hung low in the hazy, cloudless sky. Swinging northwest they rode a wide circle looking for signs, and just a short time later, Lane found the first clue, a small piece of cloth clinging down low on a mesquite limb, a piece torn from the little girl's blue, cotton dress. After taking a short while to study the trail, Lane put an easy spur to his horse and rode with one eye on the distant horizon while the other searched along the ground for more signs.

"What are you going to do when you find 'em?" Tater asked.

"I'm going to try to arrest 'em," Lane answered, "but

I may have to kill 'em. That'll be up to them, but one way or the other I'm takin' 'em to Fort Worth."

"Sheriff, do you really think those men are just going to let you arrest 'em? You're only one man and there's three of them. And if what Olsen said is true, they're packing some pretty big iron. They'll pick us off before we ever get close enough to see 'em much less arrest 'em."

Lane knew what Tater was saying was true, and up to this point he had not decided exactly how he was going to get the job done, but glancing over he said, "that's all the more reason you should stop your yapping and help me look for signs."

They had not gone far before darkness settled upon the trail, but Lane had seen enough to know that John Olsen and his family had left a well-marked trail and even though Lane could not see the ground from atop his horse, he had a good idea of the direction from which the Olsens had traveled so he rode on, picking his way through the moonlit night.

Around midnight they drew up to let the horses rest in a scattered clump of tall oak. After loosening the cinch on both saddles, Lane walked in among an outcropping of boulders at the edge of the timber and stood while letting his eyes scan the distance, knowing in his own mind it was way too early yet to see anything, but still he let his eyes search both near and far in hopes of maybe seeing the flicker from a campfire. After a short while of not seeing anything but darkness, he took a long, ragged breath and as he let it out, he mumbled, "it's been a long time."

"It's been a long time what?" a low voice coming from behind him asked.

Lane, knowing it was Tater who was doing the asking, didn't even look around. "Since I've had to do any tracking at night," he answered.

"How in the world did you learn to do it?" Tater asked. "I can barley find my way along a boardwalk in broad daylight."

"I learned from the best," Lane replied. "Big Bear Townsend, Porter Dobbs, and Mushy Crabtree are three of the finest trackers that were ever in these parts. Of course Dobbs is dead now, but he was one fine tracker. Any one of them could track a blowing leaf across a bed of solid rock and know where it was going to end up way before the leaf did." Taking a step toward the horses, he added, "we'd better be gettin' along."

For the next few hours they rode through the night without talking. Then coming to a steep, rocky bank, Lane put a hard spur to his horse to make the climb, but just as the horse broke over the rim, a coyote came over the top from the other direction and ran square-dab between the horse's legs causing him to rear and when he did the horse lost his footing in the loose rocks and started to slide and unable to get his feet dug back into the ground, he turned over backward. Lane somehow managed on his way down to jump clear of the tumbling horse, but in doing so, landed head first in among some large rocks and the hard blow he took to his head knocked him out cold.

* * *

When he opened his eyes again it was morning and from where the sun hung in the eastern sky it was late morning. Reaching up, he rubbed at the throbbing pain in his head with his hand to find the wound had been wrapped with a bandage, then bringing his hand down he looked at his fingertips to see they were smudged with bright, red blood.

"You took a pretty hard lick," a voice said. "It's a wonder you didn't break your fool neck."

Lane rubbed at his eyes trying to clear them of the blur, then looking in the direction of the voice, he realized it was Tater who was doing the talking. "What are you still doing here?" he asked. "I figured you'd be half way to Mexico by now."

"I should be," was the answer. "But I couldn't just go off and leave you in the shape you were in. If you would have died they'd probably be after me for murder. I found a shirt there in your saddlebag and didn't think you'd mind me tying it around your head. Got the blood stopped, but it's going to be a mite sore."

"How's my horse?" Lane asked.

"Just fine," Tater answered, then pointed, "I've got him on the grass."

There was a long silence then Lane said, "Tater, I don't think you robbed any man in Fort Worth. And when we get there I'm going to do what I can to find out the truth, and furthermore, I'm going to tell the sheriff what happened here, that you had a chance to run but chose to stay and help me out."

"I'd be obliged, Sheriff. I swear they've got the wrong man. Eyewitness or not, I didn't do it."

"I believe you, Tater," Lane said putting out his hand. "Now pull me up from here so we can be on our way." When Lane was on his feet, he blinked his eyes trying to clear the fuzziness from his head, then reaching into his shirt pocket he drew out the key, and after unlocking Tater's handcuffs he said, "your gun and holster are over there in my saddlebags." Reaching up, Lane adjusted the bandage then picking up his hat he dusted it against his leg then slapped it on his still aching head.

Tater rubbed at the new found freedom in his wrists, then taking his pistol and holster from Lane's saddlebag he swung it around his hips and buckled it up. Moments later, the two men stepped into the leather stirrups, and with Lane leading the way at a canter headed north.

Around midday they rode upon the spot where the robbery had taken place. And it appeared to have happened just as John Olsen had stated. The signs showed where three horses had rode from the brush on the north side of the trail and stopped the wagon. The ground was covered thick with footprints, three sets in all, two sets were of smaller men, one wore boots and the other wore moccasins. The third set were also made by boots but were obviously left behind by a much larger man; they were wider and deeper, and Lane noticed that every time the bigger man set his foot down his spur rowels touched the ground. There were other signs too: the many dark-brown stains on the ground told all three men chewed tobacco. And a closer look at the horse tracks revealed the horse the big man was riding had a back left hoof that turned out. The two smaller men had tied their horses off to the tailboard of the wagon alongside the cow and other horse and climbed into the seat, while the bigger man had mounted his horse. Lane and Tater walked a good ways along the trail tailing their reins, and when they'd seen enough, they climbed tired and hungry back into the saddles. Now it was not so much the tracking that was the big concern; the heavily-loaded wagon was leaving ruts so deep a blind man could follow. The real concern was figuring out where they were headed and what each was doing, especially the big man. He had mounted his horse so he'd be the one watching their back trail, and from what John Olsen had said, he was the one with that big Sharps rifle.

"I sure wish I had a hot cup of coffee," Lane said as he kicked his horse into a canter.

"Me too," Tater replied. "But since you left the coffee pot and everything else back at Ponders Creek with the Olsens there's no chance of us having food or coffee until we find that wagon. And that's only if we can take it away from those fellers once we do find it."

They rode on, just stopping long enough from time to time to let the horses rest. Twice they noticed where the big man had ridden from the trail. Once he had rode to the top of a hill and sat in among an outcropping of rocks and the other time they found where he had climbed up into a tree to get a better look at their back trail. "It's not going to be easy," Tater said. "He's a smart one."

"What's not going to be easy?" Lane questioned.

"Getting close enough to take 'em with these pistols."

"We've got to out smart 'em," Lane answered with confidence. "First, we've got to figure out where they're headed and when we do we can maybe ride around and get in front of 'em, but for now I don't think they've really made up their minds where they're going, they're just going."

By mid evening Lane and Tater had found where the outlaws had made their first camp, but with the sun still high in the cloudless sky they rode on until well after dark before finally stopping to rest. At first light they mounted and headed out, but had not been on the trail long when they found where the wagon had swung north. "It's South Bend," Lane announced.

"What's South Bend?" asked Tater.

"That's where they're headed. They're going to cross the Brazos at South Bend, there at the ferry crossing, and probably head west for the Bad Lands, or maybe not," Lane said after giving it some thought. "Maybe South Bend is their destination; it might be their plan to sell the wagon and stock there."

Lane turned and rode from the trail in an east northeast direction but a little after midday he swung back west. It was his intention to ride around and maybe get in front of the wagon and then start backtracking south until he came up on them. That would also lessen the chance somewhat of riding into the sights of the Sharps rifle because Lane had the notion the man packing it would be watching their back trail and not expecting a pursuit from the north.

The two men rode west until they cut the main trail leading north to South Bend and finding no fresh wagon tracks along it they knew the wagon they sought had to be south of where they now were. Lane reined in his horse, then taking off his hat, he mopped at the sweat running down his face with a sleeve. "We're going to split up," he said. "I'll stay over here and you ride along that ridge over yonder," he said pointing west. "When we spot 'em just hold your fire until we can figure out a way to take 'em without gettin' ourselves killed." Then adjusting in the saddle Lane said, "and if I was you, Tater, I wouldn't even think 'bout running."

"I'm not going to run," Tater replied with a hard aggravated shake of his head. Then nudging his horse forward he rode off.

Lane sat watching until Tater was out of sight, then he spun his horse and started south. The sun was falling fast, and now hung low in the brassy, western sky and Lane knew the light would soon fade, giving way to darkness and the uncertainty of night.

For the better part of the next hour Lane rode south, staying to the brush and well below the skyline for he knew the men he sought would be watching for anything moving along the horizon. Suddenly catching a glimpse of something white in the hazy distance, he drew up and stood tall in the saddle to have a better look. And just as he realized it was the new canvas top on the Olsens' wagon his pulse raced. "There they are," he mumbled. But not knowing whether all three men were with the wagon, he rode on slow and easy, working his way

Showdown at Deer Creek 75

through a big patch of oak then down a short bank crossing a narrow dry creek bed at the bottom. Then turning at a right angle, he made his way to the far side of a grassy flat some hundred or so yards wide, then in behind an outcropping of large boulders. There he drew up and stepped slowly to the ground but just as he was tying his horse, the evening air came alive with gunfire. "Damn it to hell," he said through gritted teeth. "I told Tater to wait." Stepping in among the rocks, he looked out to see it wasn't Tater doing the shooting at all. There was a group of at least a half dozen fast-riding men coming from the south, but in the dim light Lane could not make out exactly how many much less who they were.

One of the outlaws at the wagon had taken cover under it and the other was on the inside and both were returning fire and every time they pulled the trigger on those big bore rifles it sounded like cannons going off. But as far as Lane could tell those were the only two; the big man with the buffalo skin coat was for the time being unaccounted for. Looking across, Lane could see Tater had moved downhill to within twenty yards of the wagon and had taken cover behind a boulder.

The men riding from the south drew their horses to a sliding stop no more than forty yards from the wagon, and all hit the ground running, some taking cover behind rocks and others behind trees. Now the only way for the two outlaws at the wagon to escape was to the north and with Lane and Tater where they were, any such attempt would surely mean their deaths. "Where is the other man?" Lane asked himself in a low voice. "The big man with the buffalo skin coat?" But before he could answer, a loud roar coming from uphill and to his left sent one of the men who had ridden from the south hard to the ground. Lane quickly glanced through the dim light in the direction of the gun shot to see nothing more than a light puff of white-gray smoke. But he instantly knew it could have only been one person doing the shooting and that was the man he wanted.

Lane slowly eased from among the rocks and started walking, hunkered down, in the direction of where he'd seen the smoke rise. He had not taken but a dozen or so steps when he saw a massive shadow coming through the brush toward him. Dropping to one knee beside a tree, Lane readied his pistol and waited for what he figured to be the third outlaw to ride into view, but that never happened. He saw me or my horse, Lane thought to himself.

Slowly pushing up to his feet, he raised his head above the brush to get a look but at that instant, there was another loud, deafening roar then the loud swoosh of the bullet as it went past and a split second later, the ring of the bullet as it ricocheted off a nearby rock. At the same moment, and no more that twenty feet away, Lane saw the bright, yellowish-blue muzzle flash. Instinctively, Lane brought up his gun and fanned two quick shots in the direction of the flash, and the two loud pops that followed told him both shots had struck the man. Where, Lane did not know, but they had both hit him somewhere. There was a low painful groan, followed by the snapping of small branches and the rustle of leaves and then a hollow thud as the man fell from his horse to the ground. Lane waited for a long moment to see if the shadow moved again and when it didn't, he started from behind cover.

Moving slowly, and using much caution, Lane worked his way around the boulders and through the tangled brush to where the massive dark shadow lay motionless, but in among the dense trees where what little evening light that remained could not penetrate, the shadow lay for the most part unrecognizable, except for the unmistakable feel of the buffalo skin coat. "I guess this is better than hanging," Lane mumbled. Turning his attention back to the bottom, he noticed the gunfire had stopped and the men had moved in on the wagon. Then he saw what he thought to be Tater Rankin walking with his hands high in the air with a man following along behind him with his gun drawn. "Sheriff, here's one more," Lane heard the man with the gun call out.

"Sheriff," Lane repeated under his breath, "by glory that's a posse." Relieved it wasn't another gang of outlaws, he quickly loaded the dead man's body over the saddle then gathering his own horse, he started down the now darkened hill. But before walking clear of the brush he stopped and called out. "Hold your fire. My name is Lane Tipton. I'm the sheriff of Deer Creek."

"Come on out," a voice called back through the night.

But it wasn't until Lane walked into the glow of the campfire that he had a face to go with the voice. The man who had spoken was a tall, thin man with a long, dropping mustache. He met Lane with his hand out. "The name's Clay Moore. I'm the sheriff of Fort Worth."

"Glad to finally meet you, Sheriff Moore," Lane said with a smile. "That there," he said pointing, "is my prisoner, Luther Rankin. I was bringing him back to Fort Worth to stand trial for robbery when we ran into a family these men had robbed of this here wagon and left 'em a-foot to die."

Sheriff Moore gave a nod. "That's how we found you; we happened upon the Olsens camped out back there on Ponders Creek. They told us about you and your prisoner coming after these men. But as far as your prisoner here is concerned," he said looking over at Tater, "he ain't wanted for nothing that I know of. I thought I sent you a telegram."

"Hard to send a telegram," Lane replied, "since we ain't got one."

After a short study of Lane's last comment the sheriff said, "maybe it was a letter. Anyway, we found another witness who identified the man who did the robbing as the very same one who said this man here did it. We've got 'im locked up right now awaiting trial. After a little hard-handed talking to, he confessed." Turning to Tater, the sheriff put out his hand and said, "sorry for all the trouble, son, but I thought for sure I sent a letter."

"That's ok, Sheriff," Tater replied with a big happy smile. "As long as it's over that's really all that matters." Then looking back in Lane's direction, he said, "and thank you, Sheriff, for believing me."

In no time there were beans, and more important, a

Showdown at Deer Creek

new pot of coffee brewing, and a short time later, they had all gathered around the fire to eat, even the deputy, who had been nicked on the leg with the Sharps rifle was getting around, not real good, but getting around nonetheless.

"The Olsens will be happy 'bout gettin' their wagon back," Lane said.

"They sure seem like fine people," Moore replied. "And that little girl is the prettiest little thing I ever did see."

"I'm just glad we happened upon 'em," Lane answered. "They would have surely died out here with no food or water."

Moore threw up a hand in the direction of the three dead men. "That big one there is Dogger Morris and the other two are his brothers. We'd been tracking 'em for better than two weeks," he said, then after taking a short time to think, he added, "I don't know what makes 'em do it. At one time, Sheriff Tipton, this land was full of such men, but over the years we've kinda done away with a bunch of 'em."

"I know what you mean, Sheriff," Lane answered. "But I know of at least one more and I've got 'im in my jail right now waitin' on the judge. His name is Blackie Getts."

"Getts," the sheriff echoed.

"Yeah, he killed an unarmed man, a drifter. Shot 'im dead with a whole passel of people standing right there to see 'im do it."

"That's a bad bunch," Moore cut in. "You should

have a poster on 'im. I know I sent you one. They had 'im in jail down at Presidio, caught 'im when his horse fell during a bank robbery, and had 'im locked up tight until his gang rode in and killed the sheriff and both his deputies. Rode right into town like they owned it, in broad daylight, and shot 'em down. They never had a chance." After a pause he asked, "you got his gang, too?"

Lane's face went blank, and a cold chill suddenly washed over him. "No," he answered. "Getts was ridin' alone." Pushing up to his feet he said, "Sheriff, if you'll see the Olsens get their wagon. I think I'll mosey on back toward Deer Creek."

Moore looked up from his coffee. "Why don't you take a couple of my men here with you? If Blackie's gang is running loose and you've got Blackie in jail, you'll probably need 'em." Flipping the last of the coffee from the cup he added, "Son, you'd better watch yourself, and don't take 'em lightly. Those are some bad *hombres,* cold blooded killers of the worst kind."

"Much obliged, but there's no need. I've got my deputy, and there's a man or two there in town I can call on if I need 'em." Lane put out his hand to his former prisoner and said, "I'm glad it worked out this way, Tater."

"Me too," Rankin replied.

Turning back, Lane said, "Sheriff, I left my long-gun with the Olsens. You wouldn't happen to have one I might borrow?"

"Sure do," was the answer. Reaching over, he took up his own rifle and pitched it to Lane. "I'll get it back

Showdown at Deer Creek

from you the next time I'm in Deer Creek, or you can bring it with you the next time you come to Fort Worth."

"I'll sure do that," Lane replied. Then crossing to the wagon, he quickly found some coffee, a few cans of beans, and a small pan and added them to his saddlebags. But as he was saddling his horse, he noticed Tater was saddling his horse, too. "Where do you think you're going?" he asked.

Tater looked over at him and said, "Sheriff, when you and your deputy arrested me that night in the saloon I had just ordered and paid for a drink, but I didn't get to drink it before y'all drug me off to jail. So I think I'll ride on back and get what's owed me."

"We may be ridin' into a heap of trouble," Lane replied.

"That might be," Tater answered, "but my poor old pappy would turn over in his grave if he knew I paid for a beer I didn't drink."

Lane pulled the cinch tight, then stepping into the leather stirrups, he tipped his hat to the sheriff, then swinging the horse south, he looked over at Tater Rankin and said, "Ok, let's ride."

Unlike the night before, there was no moon to light the way, and very few stars could be seen. From the west a pack of coyotes yapped over a fresh kill, and high in the tree above an old owl hooted and took wing as the two dark shadows rode past.

Lane knew Deer Creek lay almost due south from where they now rode, and he also knew it would take at least two, maybe three days of hard riding to get there. The horses had already been a long way over some mighty rough country on little rest, and pushing them beyond their limits would only leave him and Tater on foot somewhere. But still Lane felt an overwhelming urgency to get back to Deer Creek, back to the people, back to Becky Townsend. And what about Tom Walker, Lane thought to himself as he rode. Did he still have control of the town or had Blackie's gang rode in and killed him as they had the sheriff and his deputies down at Presidio. To these questions Lane had no answers and he would have none until he got back to Deer Creek.

Chapter Four

To the distant east the sun was just starting its long, unstoppable climb toward the heavens, its dim glow fighting with the night, bringing a peaceful gray haze to the darkness, but it too, would soon give way to the rising sun that would bring the bright light of day and later the heat.

For Becky Townsend and the other captives, this night had been no different than the night before or the night before that. Her blood-shot eyes hurt from lack of sleep, and her joints and muscles ached from sitting so long in one place. The only standing or walking any of them were allowed to do at any time was a fast trip to the outhouse out behind the Double Deuce Saloon and only then under close guard. Becky rubbed at the numbness in her legs with an easy hand and as the circulation returned, the painful tingle subsided. Slowly she raised her arms high above her head and at the same time arched her back first one way, then the other, trying to ease some of the tightness. Even in the cool of the early morning, the inside of the saloon was already hot. The air was still, and with so many people sitting around so close together, it hung heavy with the smell of stale sweat. Reaching up with both hands, she slowly pushed her long, red hair back from her beautiful face then mopped the sweat from her brow with a sleeve. Slowly, she let her eyes drift over the people who sat crowded around her. For the most part they sat with their heads hung low and their eyes cast toward the floor, and when one would for some reason happen to look up, Becky saw only fear and doubt in their eyes. On the far side, near the bar, Sam Stovall sat alongside Mrs. Mahony and on the other side of her, the two kids lay sound asleep. Sam gave his head a faint nod to let Becky know he was awake, but did not speak for he knew, as everyone else did, that any sound would bring a gun barrel down on their heads. But over the past two days they had gotten in enough scattered conversation that Becky knew that Red the barkeeper was dead and so were Tom Walker, Lamar Tuggle and Evret McNare. And just before dark last night Blackie and R.C. dragged the badly injured Mr. Scott screaming and kicking from the saloon, and a short time later, the two outlaws returned with a sack of money but Mr. Scott was not with them, and he had not been seen or heard from since. No one knew for sure, but all figured he had somehow met with an ill fate.

Suddenly, the batwing doors opened and Becky looked up to see Tatum Stillwell walk through.

Just inside he stopped and drew the brown derby

Showdown at Deer Creek

from his head. For the longest time he stood rolling the derby in his hands, all the while staring across at Becky. It was a long, unsettling stare that went well beyond her outer beauty, a stare that went deep into her mind and soul. She tried desperately not to show the fear that had suddenly washed over her, but it was not to be, and the attempt only seemed to make the funny-looking old man in the brown derby hat want her even more.

"You got my part of the bank money?" he said in a loud, hateful voice.

The sound of the man speaking shot an instant fear over Becky, and almost made her stomach turn, and it was then she suddenly realized she was more afraid of this man than she had ever been of any man or anything in her life. She knew too, if given the opportunity, this man would act on his thoughts, and if she was still alive at the end, she'd even have more reason to fear him.

"Why," Blackie asked looking up from his drink, "you in some kind of big hurry to go somewhere?"

"No, it's nothing like that, Blackie," Stillwell answered while making his way slowly across the room. "But if it's my money, and if you have it split up, then I think I should have it." After a short pause he added, "Hank and Bull say they've already got their cut."

"That's right they do," Blackie snapped back, "and there's your part," he said, pointing to a stack of money on the table. "Better than two thousand each." Then with a nod of satisfaction, he added, "that's a pretty good haul for a town of this size."

"Two thousand," Stillwell repeated as he dropped to the chair across from Blackie, then looking over he said, "that's a lot of money." Then he added, "you can have it, Blackie, you can have it all, every last cent, and my saddle and horse too, if you want it. You can have everything I own for the girl."

Blackie gave the table a hard, disgusted slap and at the same instant pushed up to his feet. "Damn it, Stillwell," he yelled, "how many times do I have to tell you no—no—no. You can't have the girl, and she ain't for sale. And if she was, I for sure wouldn't sell her to you."

"You act like I'm going to hurt her, Blackie. I'm not going to hurt her. All I want is a little taste, that's all. When I bring her back she'll be good as new, not a scratch on her, I swear."

"That's what you told me about that Mexican girl down in Ojinaga, and remember you used those very same words when I let you have that pretty little thing in Coyame. And if you're having trouble remembering those two, just think back a week or so to what you did to that woman just south of here. Almost cut her head clean off, if it hadn't been for her neck bone you would have, too. No, you don't get along with women, Tatum, and I'm not going to let you kill this one. I'm goin' to sell this one back to her pappy for a nice little stake, say five maybe ten thousand dollars."

"Blackie, you know those three were different," Stillwell replied bitterly. "That one in Ojinaga kept going on about how her husband and brothers were

Showdown at Deer Creek

going to kill me. And that one in Coyame laughed at me, she just outright laughed at me. And that dirt farmer's wife is better off dead, she would have never made it without her man and boy, and if she was here right now I bet she'd probably thank me for puttin' her out of her misery."

"If I knew a woman that wouldn't laugh at you," Blackie broke in, "I'd kill her myself. And I have no doubt you're right about the farmer's wife. She probably would thank you for killing her after you'd put your filthy hands on her, and I figure she'd done it herself if you would have just given her the knife."

"What do you mean by that?" Tatum asked while slowly sliding his chair back.

Blackie gave his head a slow, unbelieving shake. "I've seen hogs that were smarter than you, Stillwell," he said, "and the answer is still no, and if you ask me again tomorrow it will still be no. What you need to do is get that girl over there out of your head." Then he added, "now get back out there and keep watch, her daddy or that do-good sheriff will be coming along anytime."

Stillwell looked hard into Blackie's eyes and said, "I don't know what difference it makes. We're going to kill 'em anyway, ain't we? R.C. told me we were going to kill 'em all then turn the town into a pile of ashes before we light out of here."

Blackie quickly looked in the direction of the captives hoping they hadn't heard, but realizing they had, he turned back to Stillwell. "You ignorant fool," he said through gritted teeth. "Shut your mouth," then throwing his coattail back, he positioned his hand over the butt of his six-gun. "I'm tired of jawin' with you, Tatum. Now either fill your hand, or pick up your money there and get out the door, or keep on sittin' there and I'll have R.C. over there drag you out feet first after I shoot you dead. Now, what's it goin' to be, Stillwell?" Blackie asked, then said, "it's up to you. It's your call."

Tatum's eyes locked on Blackie's, but he knew for a fact he could not take Blackie Getts in an even-up, face-to-face shootout. Over the years Blackie had proven time and time again how fast he was with his six-gun, and Tatum knew he was nowhere near fast enough. He knew too, if he did get lucky and somehow did manage to outdraw Blackie, R.C. Jacobs would surely kill him.

"Shucks, Blackie," Tatum finally said, "as pretty as she is, and as much as I'd like to have her, she ain't worth me and you having words. I didn't know you were goin' to sell 'er back to her pappy." Reaching over, he picked up the money from the table and after tucking it deep inside his shirt, he pushed up from the chair, slapped the derby on, turned and walked slowly toward the doors. Just before making his exit, he looked straight at Becky and said in a low voice, "it's not over yet pretty thing. I'll have you before this deal is done." Then he gave her a wink, followed by another disgusting stare that was cut short when he noticed Getts was still watching. Pushing open the batwing doors, he gave Getts another quick look of contempt, then stormed out.

Showdown at Deer Creek

Blackie looked over at R.C. and said, "I'm goin' to have to kill 'im. I can tell you that right now. I'm goin' to have to kill 'im over that girl."

"Maybe not," R.C. replied. "But if you do, it's not like you ain't give 'im fair warning. You know, Blackie, he would kill her if you sold her to 'im."

"I know," Blackie replied, "and she ain't worth nothing to me dead."

Becky watched Tatum go and when he had she felt much relief, but knew by the way her hands were shaking she was scared. She blinked her eyes trying to clear her mind of the image of the old man staring at her, but as hard as she tried, that awful picture remained, his ugly face and that disgusting wink was still there. But right now she had more important things at hand; she had heard them say all would die, but that was nothing she didn't already expect because she knew Blackie and his gang could not afford to leave anyone alive who could or would identify them and that meant killing everyone, even the children. She had heard them also say they expected her pa and Lane to be showing up before long and they were right. For she knew Lane would be getting back from Fort Worth at anytime and not knowing the town had been taken over, he might just ride in unaware of the danger and be shot down in cold blood.

But on the other hand, she knew Lane to be a smart man who didn't do much of anything without reading the signs first, looking ahead. But if he was longing to see her as much as she was longing to see him, he might not notice the streets of Deer Creek were empty, that no horses stood tied at any of the hitch rails, and no people were walking along the boardwalk. But surely he would, for Lane Tipton knew Deer Creek as well as anyone, and he knew all the people who lived here, where they should be and at what time of the day they should be there. No, it was not Lane she had to worry about, the one she really needed to be worry about was her pa. But she did not expect him for at least two more days, because that's when he'd come looking to see why she hadn't come home when she was supposed to. Unless, she thought to herself, he happens to ride in for some other reason, and if he did come in early, would he ride in by himself as he sometimes did or would he have Zack and Uncle Mushy, and maybe even some of the other men with him?

"Hey, I'm getting hungry, and I could sure use a hot cup of coffee," Blackie announced, then getting to his feet, he looked at Mrs. Mahony and said, "you and that old windbag there go make some coffee, and fix up a little something to eat."

"What have you people done with my husband?" Mrs. Scott asked.

"You need not worry about your husband," Blackie answered with a smirk. "He's doing just fine. All you need to be worried about is doing as you're told, and that is, go with that old hag there and get us something to eat."

Mrs. Mahony stood, and reaching over, she took Mrs. Scott by the hand, then leading the way they started for the door.

"You two don't get any funny ideas. If you do,"

Blackie said, "I'll give you both to old Tatum and if that ain't enough to keep you in line, just think 'bout me giving him that little girl there."

"No. Please. Don't hurt my baby!" Mrs. Mahony cried out.

Blackie laughed. "Well then, you better do as I say, and you better be quick about it."

"Ok, Ok." Mrs. Mahony answered with tears streaming from her eyes. "I'll do whatever you say. But please, Mr. Getts, I'm beggin' you. Please don't hurt my babies."

Blackie let out a big, roaring belly laugh and said, "Mr. Getts. Now that's more like it. You're kinda talking like you've got some wit 'bout you."

"Why don't you just let the women and children go?" Sam cut in.

"Let 'em go," Blackie echoed. "Now why would I go and do something silly like that? Only a dim-witted, crazy fool would be that stupid."

"Well," Sam began. "I know all you're waiting on is the sheriff to get back so you can kill 'im, but Lane Tipton ain't no fool, Getts, and if he don't see people moving 'bout the town he's going to get suspicious."

"Don't forget 'bout that other loudmouth," Blackie cut in. "That cowboy, that Mushy Crabtree fellow. He'll be dead before I leave here too, good and dead. I'm going to teach 'im better than to put his nose where it don't belong."

Sam shook his head. "Ain't neither one 'em going to ride in here if the streets are empty. Think 'bout it, Blackie. You wouldn't either."

Hearing what Sam was saying, Becky cleared her throat to get his attention and when she had, she faintly shook her head from side to side and slowly put a finger up to her lips for quiet.

But as if he had not noticed what Becky was trying to tell him, Sam said, "you might even think 'bout saddling a few horses and tying them to the hitch rails along the street, and maybe even hitching up a buggy or two. That way it would appear to anyone who knows the town and who might be watching from a distance that there's nothing wrong."

"Why are you tellin' me this?" Blackie questioned. "I thought you and that do-good sheriff were friends."

"Oh, I like 'im. Don't get me wrong," Sam answered. "But I'm just ready to have this deal over with. After you kill him and Crabtree, you and your men can be on your way and the town can get back to normal."

"Sam, shut up." Becky blurted out, almost on the verge of crying. "You don't know what you're saying. Do you realize you're helping sign Lane and Mushy's death warrants and probably Pa's, too?"

Sam looked in the direction of the teary-eyed Becky, but did not speak.

"You know, he might be right," Blackie said turning to R.C.

"Have you given some thought to how we're going to watch after all these people after we turn 'em loose?" R.C. asked. "What's goin' to keep 'em from grabbing one of those horses and hightailing it out of here?"

"Ain't nobody ridin' nowhere," Blackie blurted out. "The horses will be hobbled, and if any of these fine folks even get within reach, I want you to shoot 'em." He paused to think then added, "we can put a man up high on each end of town with a rifle just in case someone tries something and if they do, then that'll be their mistake." Turning back to Sam, Blackie said, "that's some good thinking. I like a man that uses his head."

"Sam," Becky cried out, "I can't believe you're doing this."

Sam, having a good idea of what Becky and the rest of the folks must be thinking, looked in their direction and gave his shoulders a shrug, then dropped his eyes to the floor. He knew nothing he could say now that would overshadow what he had just done, and anything he did say might tip his hand to Blackie. But for now he only knew that to all these fine, wonderful people who he had worked and lived with for so many years he was a traitor. And he had done the unthinkable; he had given Blackie Getts all the information needed to set a trap for Lane Tipton and Mushy Crabtree. A trap either man would most likely ride into without thinking, a trap that would cost them their lives.

With the plan set, it didn't take long to saddle a few horses and hitch up a buckboard or two, and with that done the towns folk were released with the instructions to mingle about town as they normally would, all that is except for Becky and Sam, who Blackie insisted on staying in the saloon with him. Then came something no one had expected. Blackie gave R.C. the order to go to the bank and let Mr. Scott out of the vault where he'd been left the night before.

When R.C. had gone, Sam walked to the window and

looked out onto the street and after a moment of studying the situation he turned to Blackie and said, "there's something not right. There's something out of place or not yet in place." He turned back to the window and looked out again and after a long, studying look he said, "I know what it is, it's the mules."

"Mules, what mules, what are you talking about?" Blackie asked.

"The mules over at the livery stable," Sam said throwing up a pointing hand. "They're still in the barn. Anyone who's ever been in this town for more than a day or two knows Evret McNare thought more of those four old mules than he did his own wife and the first thing after feeding 'em grain ever morning he'd let 'em out and fill their manger with hay. He'd flip put the mules in the east side of the corral and the horses in the west side. If Lane happens to notice those mules are still in the barn or in the corral on the west side he's going to know right off that something's wrong."

Blackie looked quickly at Sam through suspicious eyes. "East side, huh? Are you sure the mules go on the east side?"

Knowing full well that Evret McNare always put what he considered to be his prize mules on the east side so the barn would shade them from the evening sun, but hoping Blackie would think he was lying and put them on the west side and by doing so, maybe alerting Lane of something being wrong. Sam's face flushed with the question and after a moment of silence he said, "yes, I am. Matter fact, I'd stake my life on it. The mules go on the east side, horses on the west."

Showdown at Deer Creek 95

"That might be what you're doing," Blackie said with a smirk. "Bettin' your life on it." Turning to Becky he asked, "Little Missy, is the saddle maker here tellin' me true? Do the mules go on the east side of the corral?"

Becky, finally realizing what Sam was trying to do and knowing Blackie would never believe anything she said, answered, "yes, Sam's right. Mr. McNare always put the mules on the east side of the corral so the barn would give 'em some shade from the evening sun."

Blackie slowly shook his head, then all of a sudden as if someone had slapped him in the face, his eyes narrowed and as he started in Sam's direction, he dropped his hand for his six-gun and said, "what do you take me for some kind of dimwit—east side?" As he got within reach, he swung, but Sam saw it coming and ducked and Blackie missed, but on the back swing the gun barrel caught Sam solidly on the side of his head just above the right ear and the blow sent him hard to the floor. "I should shoot you," Blackie screamed, standing over Sam with his gun drawn. Then looking over at Becky with eyes filled red with hatred, he said, "I should shoot both of you graveyard dead right here and now. Did you think for a minute I wouldn't catch on to what you two were up to?" Then taking a couple of steps toward Becky, he added, "you try anything like that again and I swear, I'll kill the saddle maker and I'll give you to Tatum." He motioned with the gun barrel, "now both of you get over there and sit at that table yonder, and I don't want to hear another lying word from either of you." Turning to Hank, he said, "go across to the livery and let those mules out, and make sure you put 'em in the lot on the west side." Then looking back in the direction of Sam and Becky he gave a big satisfying smile and said, "east side. Did you two really think I'd fall for that? Y'all must think I'm crazy. On your best day you can't outsmart me, and the sooner you realize it the better off you'll be, and the longer you'll live."

As Hank went out, Mrs. Mahony walked in carrying a pot of stew in one hand, and a big pan of pone bread in the other, and Mrs. Scott followed along behind carrying several cups and a pot of hot coffee.

"It's 'bout time," Blackie called out from across the room, and then dropping into the chair he had occupied for the last three days he waited for her to fill a plate and when she had, Mrs. Scott poured coffee into a cup and placed it on the table. Then crossing to where Becky and Sam sat, they gave them food and coffee and with that done, both women turned without speaking and walked hurriedly out the door. Blackie watched after them and when they were out of sight he began to eat, but never for long at any given time did he take his eyes off the horses tied at the hitch rails, or the buckboards, or the people walking along the street.

It was obvious to Becky and Sam, too that by the way Blackie kept jerking his head at sound and dropping his hand for the butt of his six-gun at the slightest movement that he was growing restless. And they knew when a man of his caliber got restless it only made him that much more dangerous. They knew too, after what had just happened between them and Blackie, they were both very lucky to still be alive. But both realized they were not out of the woods just yet because it was clear it would take very little to set Blackie off on one of his killing sprees. But for now at least, with the townsfolk out and about and away from the killers intimidating looks and rude remarks, they felt as though they'd done some kind of good. A deed that might well keep someone from getting killed, and on top of that, they had managed to get the mules put in the wrong side of the corral, something Lane or Bear would hopefully notice from a distance and not just come riding into town unaware of the danger and helplessly gunned down in the street.

Suddenly the doors pushed opened and a much out of breath Bull Ansel stumbled through. Stopping just inside, he let his eyes quickly search the room and once he had located Getts sitting at the table, he threw up a hand toward the east and said, "Rider comin'."

Blackie instantly dropped his fork and in the same motion pushed up from the table. "Now we'll see who gets the last laugh," he said as he started for the door.

At the man's words a sudden wave of fear washed over Becky. Her pulse quickened, and her heart began pounding as though it was trying to pop from her chest, but none of that was more prevalent than the saddle size lump that had suddenly caught in her throat. For she knew someone she loved more than life itself was probably about to die. Then came the awful feeling of helplessness, for she also knew there was absolutely nothing she or anyone else could do to stop it. Or was there? I can scream, she thought to herself. *I can scream out to warn them, but if they're close enough to hear me it will already be too late*. She glanced at the two men standing by the door who stood with their backs turned, then letting her eyes move slowly down she focused on their holsters. If I can just get my hands on one of those guns, she thought. *I might not get them all, but I could certainly make a showing.* Acting mostly on instinct mixed with fear, she started to push up from the table when a hand suddenly stopped her.

"Not yet," Sam whispered. "Let's wait and see if one of 'em goes out."

Becky did not at first understand Sam's reluctance, but finally realized he was right, if one of the outlaws did walk outside, the chances of them overpowering the one that remained before he knew what was happening would be much greater. She gave her head an agreeing nod and relaxed back into the chair.

The boardwalk suddenly came alive with footsteps as the towns folk realized someone on horseback was approaching the town and thinking there would surely be gun-play, they hurried to get somewhere safe.

Then came a sound that was louder and more deafening than anything Becky had ever heard in her life and with each passing moment, it seem to grow even louder. It was a heartbreaking, terrifying sound that sent one cold shiver after another up her spine. For she knew at the end someone would probably die because the sound she was hearing was the awful sound of quiet and it had fallen over the whole town. Even the old sign that hung down from chains above the door of the Double Deuce was silent and she couldn't ever remember it not squeaking.

Knowing time was quickly running out for whoever

was riding into town, Becky looked over at Sam hoping for some kind of a sign he was ready to attack, but instead, he just faintly moved his head from side to side, then gesturing with a hand to three empty whiskey bottles setting on a nearby table, he whispered, "when I give the word, fill your hands when you go by."

A dog barking drew Becky's attention toward the door first then the window, but she was still unable to see anything except the empty street. She knew it had to be the old spotted dog that stayed around the livery stable because he was the only dog in town, and from the sound of his bark, the rider had to be coming from the east and had to be about at the livery stable. And the old dog had greeted whoever it was as he did everyone who had ridden into town over the past five years, with a friendly bark and a happy wag of his tail. But she also knew that the east was the direction Lane would be riding from and the thought frightened her. Again she looked at Sam, but he, like the times before, just shook his head no. And even though it angered her for him to sit there doing nothing, she knew he was right, for they would stand little if any chance against two men with guns. But I've got to try, she thought to herself. *I just can't let them shoot Lane down in cold blood and if they kill me trying to stop them, then so be it because I know I'd rather die trying to help Lane than to try to live one day knowing I didn't do anything.* She looked across the saloon and saw that both men were still standing with their backs turned. Glancing at Sam she whispered, "I'm going with or without you." Then casting her eyes to the three empty bottles she drew deep and long from her inner well of courage, but just as she started to stand, she heard Getts say, "I don't know who it is, but it sure ain't that loudmouth, sheriff."

"Do you want us to kill 'im?" R.C. asked.

"No," Getts answered. "He's probably just some cowhand passin' through, and anyway if the sheriff is close, and he sure might be, he would most likely hear the shot."

"We don't have to shoot 'im," R.C. answered.

"Put the knife away, R.C.," Getts replied in a whisper. "We'll just take his gun and put 'im in here with the other two," Getts paused then said, "that is unless he wants to try to be a hero or cause us some trouble, and if he does then you can kill 'im, R.C."

Hearing Blackie say it wasn't Lane brought a faint smile to Becky's face and a low "thank God," fell from her lips. But the joy was short-lived as she tried to think of who the lone rider could be. Was it her pa who had maybe sensed something being wrong and was riding in from the east trying to fool someone? Or maybe it was her Uncle Mushy, or maybe it was like Blackie said and it was just some drifter passing through. But before she could sort through her many thoughts she heard something that told her she would soon know, for now she could hear the sound of horse hooves against the hard ground as the rider made his way along the street. She let her eyes move quickly to the window just as the horse and rider passed into view, but the mere glimpse she got didn't reveal much more than a man wearing a black hat, and a long canvas duster, but it was enough so she could tell it was definitely no one she knew.

"Howdy," the man said as he drew up.

R.C. walked to where Becky could just barely see him over the top of the batwing doors. "What can we do for you, mister?" he asked.

"Just a-thinking about maybe wettin' my throat," the stranger answered. Then motioning in the direction in which he'd rode he said, "I'm a mite dry, been a long, hot, dusty trail."

"What trail is that?" R.C. asked.

There was a long pause, but when the stranger spoke again his voice was loud and clear. "I don't see you wearin' a star, mister, and if I did, where I've been or where I'm headed ain't really none of your concern. I just kinda ride where the trail takes me, and along the way I try not to ask any questions and by doing that I don't find myself havin' to answer many."

"You might not answer any questions," Blackie said, pushing halfway through the door, "but I can tell you this that if you reach for that six-shooter you're wearing I'll bet you're dead before you touch it. There's two rifles pointin' at you right now and they're just waiting to blow your smart mouthed head off."

"Blackie Getts, is that you?" the stranger asked.

Surprised by the question, Blackie stopped in his tracks, then looking up at the man he asked, "do I know you?"

"No, I don't figger you do and I don't really know you, but I've seen your face on enough wanted posters

I knew who you were the second you opened that door. The name's Truitt, Mr. Getts, Truitt Putman. I've been riding down south with Charlie Hennessey."

"Charlie Hennessey," Blackie echoed. "What in the world has that old mangy coyote been up to?" Then quickly letting his eyes scan the distant horizon he asked, "where's he at? Is he with you?"

"No, he's not. And he ain't doing nothing," the stranger replied. "Charlie's dead. He got done in down at Laredo during a bank job. They killed Mutt Brown and Johnny Gates, too. And that Mexican, Manuel Salazar, he hadn't been ridin' with us but two weeks when he took a bad one in his gut. The last time I seen him, he was sittin' slumped in the saddle right in the middle of the Rio Grand River. I'm a-thinking he's probably dead by now, too. But me, I swung north and worked my way up through San Antonio and Waco to Fort Worth."

"Fort Worth?" Blackie questioned. "If you were headed north, what brings you here from Fort Worth?"

"Looking for a man by the name of Dogger Morris," Putman answered. "You heard of 'im?"

Blackie shook his head and said, "can't say that I have. Who is he? Where's he from?"

Putman gave his shoulders an unknowing shrug. "I don't rightly know. I heard 'bout 'im in Fort Worth. They say he's a buffalo hunter, or used to be. They say he's meaner than all get out. They say he's got a little gang together and doin' pretty well for himself. I was kinda figgerin' on seenin' if I could find 'im and maybe hookin' up."

Showdown at Deer Creek 103

Blackie liked the way this Truitt Putman was talking, and it was obvious he knew what he was talking about, and knowing he might soon be needing a new gun himself if Tatum kept running his mouth, he looked at the newcomer and said, "well, get down and come on in, 'cause if you think I'm goin' to bring that drink out here to you, you've got another thing coming."

"Why, thank you, Mr. Getts," Putman said with a big smile, then stepping to the ground, he tied his horse and after loosening the cinch, made his way up the steps slowly toward the door.

He was a tall, lean made man with thin, steel-gray eyes and a full shock of black hair that hung down well past his collar, and his face was covered with better than a week's growth of black stubble. He wore a full length canvas duster that was covered thick with trail dust and a newly cleaned six-gun that he wore low and tied to his right leg.

Becky looked over at Sam and in a low voice said, "we waited too long, it's too late now."

Sam looked deep into her beautiful green eyes and said, "think about it, Rebecca. They said they weren't going to kill 'im, and Getts never went all the way out the door. From where he stood he could have shot the both of us before we got halfway across the room, much less to 'im." Then leaning closer he added, "I know you're wantin' to stop this deal, to do something to help out. I do too, but there's no need in us getting ourselves killed when it would serve no real purpose at all. Now you just slow down and think about it."

Becky, knowing full well Sam was right, nodded and

started to speak but before she could say anything, the batwing doors squeaked loudly and she looked in that direction to see Blackie turn back inside and behind him walked the newcomer and following along after him was R.C. Jacobs. The three men entered and after they had, Bull went out.

"Have a seat," Blackie said to Truitt. Then directing the newcomer to a chair with a pointing hand, he added, "I'll see about gettin' us a fresh bottle."

But noticing Sam and Becky, Truitt asked, "what have we got here?"

"Oh," Blackie started to say, "that's the town's saddle maker, and that girl there, well, she's kinda my hold card. You see she's the daughter of a cattle rancher who has a big spread out west of town here a few miles. I'm a figgerin' her pappy will pay a small fortune to get her back. That is, if he has anything left. We've already cleaned out the bank and I've got the notion that most of what we took belonged to him."

"She's a right pretty little thing, ain't she?" Truitt remarked. "I know one thing, Blackie," he said with a smile, "if her pa don't want to pay, I know a Mexican down in Matamoros that will give you top dollar. Yes, sir, old Salvador would really like that light skin and red hair."

"Come on over and have a seat," Blackie said as he filled the glasses. "I'm not talking about sellin' her for no two hundred dollars so some Mexican can make her a whore, Truitt. No, I'm talking about big money, say five, maybe even ten thousand dollars."

"Ain't no man in his right mind going to pay you

Showdown at Deer Creek

money like that for no woman," Truitt answered as he dropped down into the chair across from Blackie.

"I'm not talking about just any man, Truitt," Blackie said with a smile. "No, I'm not. I'm talking about her daddy. And I say he will if he has it." Blackie looked out onto the street and noticing it was empty of people, turned to R.C. and said, "you better go get the folks moving about the street again. That sheriff should be showing up anytime and we don't want him gettin' suspicious before he rides in here."

"Sheriff," Truitt echoed, "what sheriff?"

"That damn do-gooder sheriff of this town who made the mistake of his life when he locked me up, that's what sheriff, and I'm waitin' to shoot him dead for doing it," Blackie answered. "No man locks Blackie Getts up and lives to tell about it. No man."

Truitt Putman forced a half-hearted laugh at Blackie's remark and said, "Charlie always said you were no one to mess with, Blackie. We all heard about that deal down at Presidio. For weeks the border was crawlin' so thick with lawmen lookin' for you we had to lay low."

"Well," Blackie began, "they didn't find me now did they? And do you know why they didn't find me, Truitt? They didn't find me because I'm smarter than they are. They're looking for me down there and I'm way up here."

Truitt gave his head a nod, then looking over the rim of the empty glass he asked, "how 'bout me maybe hookin' up with you, Blackie? I'm good with my gun and I'm known for doing whatever it takes to get the job done."

"I know you're a good man, Truitt, or Charlie Hennessey would have never let you ride with him, but I've got a full crew." Then after taking a short time to think Blackie said, "let me give it some thought, but for now you're sure welcome to hang around. Who knows, by the time this deal is done I may be a man or two short."

"Much obliged," Truitt said. Then setting the glass down on the table he got to his feet and said, "it's been a day or two since I've had anything but jerky and that plate of stew there looks awful good. I think I'll go see if I can rustle me up a little something to eat."

"You won't have to look far, and it won't cost you a penny," Blackie replied. "Just go across to the café and tell that old windbag over there you want some grub and to put it on my bill."

Becky watched the newcomer walk out the door leaving only Blackie to watch after her and Sam, but Blackie had taken up his plate and turned his chair so he was looking straight at them, and she knew that any move they made would be fatal. But soon things would change and Becky knew it, for at any moment Lane or her pa would be riding into town. There would be shooting and death upon the streets of Deer Creek. And now, as though things weren't already bad enough with five cold blooded killers in town, apparently there was yet another.

Chapter Five

Bear Townsend had moved from his study out onto the porch to get away from the paperwork for a while and to give his eyes a little rest. And even though he tried hard not to, it seemed like every time he sat down in that old swing he dozed off to sleep. The sound of the door opening brought him from his evening slumber and he looked in the direction of the disturbance to see Carmen coming with the coffee pot. "I must've drifted off," he said as she approached.

"*Sí, Señor* Townsend, you were tired."

"Not so much tired, Carmen. It's my eyes, they're no good anymore. They seem to hurt and water all the time and even more so when I'm readin' or doing something like working on the books."

"Could be you need some—some—how you say *lentes* in *inglés*. Oh you know *Señor* Townsend, some of those things . . ." But not being able to think of the word, Carmen took her hands up to her face and closing her fingers together made circles around her eyes.

"Specks," Bear guessed.

"*Sí, Señor* Townsend, specks. Maybe they would help you see better, maybe your eyes would stop making water. My father had spe—specks many years ago. I think maybe Campo must need them also. They would not help him read because he doesn't know the letters or the words. But maybe specks would help him find his way home. Sometimes when Campo goes to the cantina in town he has much trouble finding his way home until late the next day."

Bear gave a laugh, then a nod of thanks as Carmen filled his cup with the hot liquid. "*Gracias*," he said. "You know, Carmen, y'all might be right. Zack and Becky say the same thing, that I need specks. I don't guess it would hurt anything to give 'em a try. I noticed Lamar Tuggle has a whole big box of 'em there at the hardware store. I might just try looking through a pair the next time I'm in town, just to kinda see what they do."

"Who knows," Carmen said as she turned for the door, "they may be good." Then looking up to see a rider coming from the barn she mumbled, "here comes *Señor* Mushy—I bring a cup."

"Yeah, you probably should," Bear replied. "We already know he'll be wantin' to wet his whistle."

"Howdy," Mushy said as he drew up. "Thought I'd see about maybe gettin' a cup of Carmen's fine coffee.

Showdown at Deer Creek 109

You know, Bear, I think she makes a far better cup than her husband. Don't get me wrong, I'm not complaining because if it was either his or none I'd take his every time."

"I would have never guessed you'd be wantin' a cup of coffee, and yes, Carmen does boil up some mighty fine sipping . . . she sure does, she makes a fine cup of coffee," Bear answered. But knowing how nervous his old friend got when there was no coffee and seeing a chance for a good laugh he said, "but you're a tad late, Mushy," then raising his cup he added, "this here is the last of it."

"Last cup?" Mushy replied. "Well, Bear, don't you have anymore there in the house somewhere?"

"No, sir, not a bean left and won't have any until Becky gets back from town with the supplies."

"That'll be what, at least a couple more days won't it?"

"More than likely," Bear answered.

Mushy looked puzzled over the statement, then thinking he replied, "I just left the cook shack and Campo didn't say a word 'bout being out of coffee." Spinning his horse he said, "I'll ride back and see if I can find an extra sack there in the storeroom."

"Just hold up," Bear called out with a laugh. "We've got coffee. Carmen saw you coming so she's in there now gettin' you a cup. Get on down and sit a spell." Then moving from the swing into one of the chairs at the table he added, "I know that ride you just took from the cook shack to here was hard on you."

Mushy stepped to the ground and as he made his way

up the steps he shook his head and said, "Bear, you old coyote, you shouldn't josh me 'bout being out of coffee. And no, the ride from the cook shack to here didn't do me in."

"I know I shouldn't," Bear answered, "but I just couldn't see passing up the chance. Had you going, didn't I?"

But before Mushy could answer, Carmen walked from the door with a cup in one hand and the coffee pot in the other. "*Buenas tardes, Señor Mushy,*" she said with a welcoming nod.

"*Buenas tardes, mi ameno joven dama,*" Mushy replied.

The words brought a smile to Carmen's aged lips then a bashful giggle, and her eyes lit up as they most always did when Mushy was around. When she got to within reach, she gave him a playful slap on the shoulder and replied, "*Gracias, Señor* Mushy, *gracias*—thank you." Placing the cup down on the table she filled it and turned back for the door.

"What was that all about?" Bear questioned.

"Oh, nothing," Mushy answered. "She told me good evening and I said 'Good evening, my lovely young lady.' "

Bear chuckled, then looking west at the thick cloud of dust rising high above the corrals, he jerked his head in that direction and said, "I see you've got the men working on busting some of those last horses we rounded up."

"Yes, I do, and let me tell you, Bear, there's some

Showdown at Deer Creek

mighty fine animals in that bunch." Taking up the cup, he gave it a short cooling blow then a taste, then looking over the rim through the rising steam he said, "you know Becky's sure gettin' all fired up 'bout the weddin' and all ain't she?" He sipped the coffee then added, "guess it's something we need to be thinkin' 'bout too, where we're going to set up the tables and such. You know, Bear, the whole town is going to show up and I wouldn't be the first bit surprised if probably half the state."

"Ain't but one place for the tables and that's out west of the house there under those three old pecan trees," Bear answered, then his voice fell silent for several minutes and when he spoke again his words were full of doubt and uncertainty. "What do you think, Mushy? I mean 'bout her gettin' married, and Lane? Hell, she grew up with 'im."

"I know she did, and I understand what you're saying, Bear." Then propping an elbow on the table he leaned over and said, "have you looked into Becky's eyes lately? Have you noticed the change in her manners and the way she carries herself? She's not just one of the cowhands anymore, Bear. She's a young lady and from where I stand, the young lady's in love, and she just so happens to be in love with Lane Tipton, a man we both know to be one fine person and a man that will take good care of her."

"Why can't he just come back out here and help you, me and Zack take care of this place? Where did he ever get the notion to be a lawman anyway?"

"I think you have the Indians to curse for that,"

Mushy answered. "I think when the Indians killed his family and he couldn't do anything but lay under that old tree and watch kinda set him on that path."

The sudden thought of that terribly cold day so many years ago brought a somber look to Bear Townsend's face and when he spoke again his voice shook. "That had to be awful hard for that little fellow to watch, and he had those scorpions biting him, too. You remember, Mushy, his back, face and belly was covered in 'em."

"How could I forget?" Mushy replied. "No, sir, I sure wouldn't want to go through what he did."

After a long pause, Bear said, "where has the time gone? Seems like only yesterday we were teaching those kids how to ride, rope, and shoot. All four did well, but you know, Mushy, Becky was always the fastest learner out of the four and only second to Zack in riding and second to none when it came to handling a gun . . . she could out draw and out shoot any of 'em and she could almost beat 'em with her eyes closed."

"I'll have to admit she's awfully good at both," Mushy replied with a laugh. "But by me doing the teaching what else could you expect?"

"Hey," Bear snorted playfully, "I had a hand in it, too."

Mushy gave a smile and said. "You just said it, Bear. Becky's smart, awful smart and I know she's making the right decision in gettin' married."

Bear looked into the knowing eyes of his old friend for a long moment then turning, he called out, "Carmen, I think Mr. Crabtree is ready for another cup

Showdown at Deer Creek 113

of your fine coffee." Then looking back he said, "oh, I guess you're right, Mushy, but—" His words were suddenly cut short by the sound of a horse coming hard from the southwest and both men quickly stood to get a better look. "What do you make of that?" Bear asked.

"I don't know," Mushy answered, "still too far away to be sure, but it kinda looks like Zack. What in the world is he trying to do to that horse, kill 'im?"

Both men knew Zack would never use a horse in any such way unless it was a matter of life or death. They started from the porch and in the shade of the old cottonwood out front they stopped to wait. "What in the world?" Bear mumbled, then looking to Mushy he said, "I don't have a good feeling 'bout this. No, I don't, this ain't lookin' none too good at all."

At the banks of Deer Creek the rider crossed at full stride and when he topped the bank on the nearside, he started yelling and waving his arms, trying desperately to draw someone's attention.

"By heavens, Mushy, you're right. That's for sure who it is."

Moments later, the horse came to a sliding stop just inches from the two men and both reached out and grabbed hold of the reins.

Zack Townsend, like his father, was a big built man with wide shoulders, powerful arms, and big hands. He had the same dark hair and eyes his father had when he was younger, and the manner in which they conducted themselves was a whole lot the same. Both were easy going men willing to live with the hand they'd been dealt, but at the drop of a hat, either would buck a stacked deck, and when they did, they usually left cards scattered. And for a man of his size, Zack Townsend sat a saddle as well as any man and was known to be one of the top bronc busters in the country.

He looked down at his father and blurted, "They're all dead, Pa. They're every last one dead."

"Who's dead?" both men echoed at the same time.

"The Penningtons," Zack answered badly out of breath. Then sliding from his horse, he added, "all of 'em. Bill, Bernice, and Tommy. They're all dead, murdered."

"Indians?" Mushy questioned.

"Not unless Indians have started riding horses with iron on their feet."

"Speaking of horses," Bear cut in, "we need to get the saddle off of this one here so he can blow." Turning to Mushy, he handed him the reins and said, "take 'im on to the corral, make sure he gets a good rubdown and extra grain."

Mushy gave a nod then asked, "you want me to get the men ready to ride?"

"Not right yet," Bear answered. "Let me see if I can find out what's going on first. If they're already dead, there's no real need in being in a hurry." Turning for the porch he said, "come on up, Zack, I'll get Carmen to bring you some coffee." Then thinking he asked, "you hungry? How long has it been since you've had anything to eat?"

"I've had jerky, but if she's got something I'd sure take it."

A short time later the door opened and Bear walked

out with a cup of coffee and after handing it to his son, he dropped into a chair across from him. "Now," Bear said, "if it wasn't Indians doing the killing, who do you reckon did it?"

"I don't know for sure, Pa, but I'm figurin' it had to be white men or maybe even Mexicans," Zack answered. "Like I said, the horses were all shot, and I found no sign of Indians anywhere."

"Well now, just back up a little and start at the beginning."

"Ok, Pa, we had finished checking the cattle at Taylor Flats and on the way home I thought we'd swing by Indian Springs and check on the water and while there drop in on the Penningtons to see how they were getting along."

"Now, son," Bear said, not making light of the situation but trying to ease some of the pain the boy felt, "are you sure that's the real reason you went by, to check on 'em? Usually when I stop by, it isn't so much to check on 'em as it is to see if Bernice might have one of her fruit pies or some of that sugar bread cooked up. If she did, I was sure to get a slice, and she'd have it no other way. Yes, sir, Bernice Pennington was a top-hand at makin' them pies and such, and it always seemed to make her happy when someone would kick up a fuss over her cookin'," he smiled, then added, "and old Bill was a hard worker. A finer man there never was, a good husband and father, and for many years a—friend."

Zack looked over to see only sadness in the eyes of his father and after realizing Bear was making the comment to calm him down, he took a long ragged breath. "Not wanting to just ride in on a person unexpectedly and maybe getting mistaken for outlaws, we drew up on top of that rise just west of the house thinking Bill would eventually spot us and wave us in. But the longer we sat there, Pa, the more I got the notion that something was wrong. The house and barn were way too quiet and I'd seen no one moving 'bout. After a bit, we rode off the hill, but it wasn't until we started across the yard that I spotted Bill. He was lying face down about halfway between the barn and house; he'd been shot in the back three, maybe four times. I couldn't really tell because he'd been dead for quite a while and his body was in pretty bad shape. They've been dead a couple of weeks I'd guess, maybe longer."

"Don't nobody ever go by there unless they're lost. If you hadn't happened by it might have been months before someone found them." Then Bear mumbled, "And Bernice?"

Zack glanced down at his boots for a long moment and when he did finally look back up he said, "yeah, we found her there in the house, Pa. She didn't have any clothes on and she'd been badly mistreated. She'd been tied hands and feet to the bed and her throat had been slashed so bad, her head was almost cut plum off."

Bear quickly wiped at the awful paleness that had suddenly settled over his face with both hands, but hearing the sound of the door being opened, he slowly looked up to see Carmen coming with a plate of food in one hand and a glass of milk in the other.

"Here is some food, *Señor* Zack," she said as she

placed the plate on the table. "It is stew and bread and a big glass of buttermilk."

"Thank you," Zack replied with a nod then glancing up he asked, "you didn't happen to hear what we were talking about just before you came out the door did you, Ms. Carmen?"

The old woman shook her head and answered. "No, *Señor* Zack. I was working and I don't hear anything when I'm busy."

When Carmen had gone back into the house, Zack looked over at his father and said, "we liked to have never found Tommy's body, and were just about to give up when Teal found him up in the loft of the barn. He'd been shot in the face, and the whole top of his head was gone. I don't know who would do something like this, Pa, but whoever it is, they're a bad lot, and the really bad part is, it's probably not the first time they've done it and it probably won't be their last."

"It'll be their last if I find 'em," Bear answered abruptly. Then seeing Mushy coming back from the corral, Bear got to his feet and walked out to meet him. "We better head out," he said as Mushy rode up. "If you have the men saddle a couple of horses it'll just be me, you and Zack going. The Van Dill brothers are already down there. And tell Campo to load us up a few supplies. This is a bad deal, Mushy, and the sooner we take care of it the better. Oh yeah, if you ain't already done it, tell the men what we're up against and for them to keep an eye on things until we get back." Turning, Bear made his way back to the house where he found Carmen going about her work. "We'll be gone a few days," he said. "Tell

Becky when she gets back that we've gone to Indian Springs and for her to stay around the house until we return. Keep your eyes open, Carmen, we've got some bad *hombres* running loose. I'm a-figgerin' they're far from here by now, but keep your eyes open all the same."

"*Sí*, I will, *Señor* Townsend. It is bad what they did to Señora Pennington."

Bear jerked his head. "I didn't think you'd heard."

"I hear, but not good for *Señor* Zack to know I did."

"I'm obliged, Carmen," he said with an easy nod. "And yes, it is. Those were fine folks. They sure didn't deserve anything like this. Don't anybody deserve to die like that." Then making his way into his study, he took a Winchester from the rack and from the drawer, a box of cartridges and when he walked out onto the porch he noticed Mushy bringing the horses. Looking to Zack he said, "it's time to ride, son."

It was not a trip Bear Townsend was eager to make but one he knew was necessary, for someone had done the unthinkable. Someone had taken three innocent lives and whoever that someone was, under Bear Townsend's law, would have to pay for their crime. But he knew too, that before he could collect on the debt owed, he would have to find the man or men responsible and there in itself lay the big problem. If it had been two weeks since the murders, as Zack had said, Bear knew they might not ever find the trail and if that indeed turned out to be the case, the killers of his long-time friends might go unpunished. With that awful thought in mind, he stepped into leather and swung his

Showdown at Deer Creek 119

horse west. After crossing Deer Creek, he spurred the bay into a lope.

Why in the world did this have to happen, he thought to himself as he rode. Thinking back to the first time he ever laid eyes on Bill Pennington and his family, he remembered why they were living at Indian Springs and whose idea it was in the first place. And the longer he thought, the clearer his memory became until it was just like it had happened only yesterday.

Bear had just got up from a fine supper of beans, bacon and cornbread, and when Anna returned from putting the kids to bed they walked out onto the porch with their coffee cups and took a seat in the swing. Like the day before and the day before that, it was hot and it had been unusually hot for early spring, but now that the sun had settled on the western horizon and a light westerly breeze had begun to stir. It was starting to cool. They hadn't been sitting long when Anna suddenly jumped to her feet and looking east she raised a pointing hand and said, "Bear, looky yonder. There comes a wagon."

And lo and behold she was right, there was a wagon coming along the trail, and it wasn't long before it drew up in front of the house.

From the porch it only looked to be a man and woman sitting on the seat, but as they walked closer, it became clear by the bundle in her arms the young lady wearing the blue bonnet was holding a baby.

"Evening," Bear said with a welcoming wave.

"Evening," the man replied. "The name's Pennington,

Bill Pennington and this is my wife, Bernice and that baby she's holdin' is our son, Tommy."

"Glad to meet you, Bill," and with a nod to the lady Bear said, "evening Mrs. Pennington. Townsend is our name. My friends call me Bear and this here is my wife, Anna. We've got three young 'uns of our own bedded down there in the house."

"Bernice," Anna broke in, "why don't you hand me the baby and you folks come on up and rest a spell? I know you must be tired, especially traveling with a new baby. Lord, ain't this heat been dreadful? And if you're hungry, we've got beans and cornbread and I can cook up some meat."

"That sounds awful good," the man said, "but we wouldn't want to put you folks out none. We were hoping to maybe get some water for the horses."

"Don't be silly," Anna replied as Mrs. Pennington handed her the baby. Turning to her husband she said, "Bear, why don't you show Mr. Pennington where he can water his horses and I bet he might even appreciate you giving 'im a hand with 'em."

By the time the newcomers had finished their meal, Bear and Anna had learned from conversation with the two that they had traveled from Springfield, Missouri. At the time of their departure they had no real destination in mind, only to come west, but now they had the new baby and it was time to settle down somewhere. And it was while Anna and Bernice were cleaning up the kitchen and putting the dishes away that Anna invited the young family to stay the night.

Shortly after all had turned in, Anna rolled over and propping up on one elbow she said. "Bear, you know Indian Springs would be a good place for the Pennington's. He could keep the spring cleaned out, you know after every rain of any size you have to send men down there to clean the silt out where it's washed down from the hill above."

"Squatters on my land?" Bear blurted out. "Anna, do you know what you're saying? That would be giving an open invitation to every wagon passing through here. No, absolutely not. And if I did happen to say yes, the Indians would have 'em before the week was out."

"They wouldn't be squatters, Bear. You'd be giving 'em a job and they'll have to deal with the Indians no matter where they go," she said. Then she added, "If nothing else, I wish you'd give it some thought, hon." Then with a loving, little pat to his shoulder her voice fell silent.

Bear lay for a long moment staring up through the darkness at the ceiling. He knew his wife was right, that after each big rain he had to send men down to clean out the spring and if it just so happened to rain the next week, it would be time to do it all over again. Having someone living there would be a big help and would save the men from having to drop whatever they were doing to go clean it out. And it had to be cleaned out and Bear knew it because Indian Springs was the only year round water supply between Shank Corner and Taylor Flats and for it to go dry would mean a lot of thirsty cattle. "But still," he mumbled to himself in a low voice, "they'd be squatters and I'll have no part in that." Then came another loving, little pat on his shoulder and the words, "I just wish you'd give it some thought, that's all, Bear, just some thought."

He huffed over onto his side and with a rough hand, yanked the covers up. Anna had always been able to get him to do things he'd never dream of doing for another living soul, and more often than not, it only took her a few words to get him to do it. But not this time, he thought to himself. *No sir-ree-bob, it ain't going to work this time. I'll not have squatters on my land.*

After a long night of tossing and turning, and well before sunup the next morning, Bear made his way into the kitchen to find Carmen already fixing breakfast. At the table, Anna and the kids were sitting in their usual places and the Penningtons sat on the opposite side sipping coffee. Anna was holding the Penningtons' baby and the little fellow seemed to be getting most of the attention from all three of the kids. "Mornin'," Bear said and by the time he had taken a seat, Carmen had brought him coffee. "*Buenos días, Señor* Townsend," she said as she set the cup down. "*Buenos días*," Bear replied. Glancing at his wife who sat smiling at him. Bear looked over at the Penningtons and said, "I've been doin' some thinking, Bill and I've got a spring down south of here aways and ever time it rains, it covers over with silt causin' it to stop up. I was thinking 'bout maybe putting someone down there to look after it for me and to keep it cleaned out. Would you and your wife be interested in doin' anythin' like that? You've got that fine team of horses and there's an old go-devil already down there just waitin' to hitch 'em to."

Showdown at Deer Creek

Bill looked at his wife, then at Anna, then back at Bear, but before he could speak Anna said, "you should know before you make a decision that there's no house there, but I'm sure my husband, being the man he is, would see you got some good help with building one. And they'd do a fine job, too, just look at this one, They built it."

"You might have some trouble out of the Indians down that way," Bear cut in, "they've been using that spring for years. But you're going to have that no matter where you go. Over the years, they've killed a few of my men, and cattle too, but for the most part we've managed to keep 'em beat back."

"Mama, does that mean Tommy will be my little brother?" Becky asked.

The room instantly filled with laughter and when it had faded, Anna answered, "no, sweetheart. Tommy wouldn't be your little brother, but we would get to see 'im from time to time. We could go down to Indian Springs and visit with them or they could maybe come up this way and spend some time with us."

"I'd like that," Becky said with a smile.

Robert looked over at his pa and said, "we could all get in the buckboard and I could drive it down there."

"Maybe so, but you're still a tad young for that, don't you think?" Bear said, looking back at his oldest son with a grin. Then turning his attention back to Bill Pennington, he continued. "I know it's a big step, Bill, and it's not something you'd want to jump into without talking it over with your wife first, but maybe it's something for y'all to think 'bout and if you do decide to do it, all you've gotta do is let me know."

"Thank you for the offer," Bill answered, "and it is something we'll give some thought to, but it's like you said, Bear, we'd sure need to talk it over."

Two days later, Bill, Bernice, and Tommy Pennington loaded up in their wagon and, along with a fine crew of men led by Mushy Crabtree and Porter Dobbs, headed south for Indian Springs. And since that time it had proven over and over again through the years to be one of the best decisions Bear Townsend had ever made, and he knew if not for Anna giving him the idea, it was a decision he would have never made. His beautiful Anna, his beautiful, beautiful Anna. "God, how I miss you," he mumbled in a low voice.

"Pa—Pa—look out, Pa," he heard Zack call out. And the loud words brought him back from his thoughts just in time to realize he was heading straight for a ravine. "Whoa," Bear said as he drew up hard on the reins and when the horse had slid to a stop, Bear turned in the saddle and looking back at Zack he said, "I'm glad you were watching out for me, son 'cause I was sure fixin' to ride off in there." Then giving his head a hard, aggravated shake, he swung the horse at left angle and rode on, but this time with his mind less on the deaths of the Penningtons and more on the dangers of the trail.

To the west the sun was slowly dropping below the blueness of the distant horizon and its bright, golden rays, like long pointed fingers, streaked the far off sky. To the east thin, white, wispy clouds drifted aimlessly along, and beneath them a red-tailed hawk, with his wings motionless, rode a current of wind. Bear cast his eyes upon all the natural beauty and knew that if not for the awful circumstance in which they rode, it would be the perfect end to an otherwise beautiful day.

"We might want to be thinking 'bout maybe finding a place to make camp," Mushy said from behind.

"That sounds like a good idea," Zack agreed.

Hearing the conversation between the two men, Bear drew up and as they rode alongside he said, "maybe so. We've covered a lot of ground in a short amount of time, and the horses are startin' to wear, no need ridin' 'em down." Standing tall in the saddle, he let his eyes quickly survey the countryside looking for a place to make camp, but he knew it couldn't just be any place it had to be a place with cover, a place hopefully where he'd have a clear view in all directions. Even though he figured the killers of the Penningtons to be long gone by now, he'd been wrong before and if they weren't, he wanted to be ready and if the killers were gone, they still had Indians to think about. Spotting a grove of trees atop a not too distant rise, he threw up a pointing hand and said, "over yonder in that small stand of oak might be a good place." Then nudging his horse forward, he led the way through the mesquite and scattered scrub cedar in that direction.

They were not long in stripping the saddles from the backs of the tired horses, but not wanting to take a chance on someone maybe being close by and hearing the picket-pens being driven into the hard ground, they put the hobbles on. With that done, Mushy began gathering wood, while Zack scooped out a hole in the earth. Then placing the wood down in it, they started a small fire that for the most part could not be seen from any direction except above. A pot of coffee was started, and while it brewed, Zack cut the top from a can of beans and Mushy sliced bacon into a skillet. As they were doing that, Bear stood guard at the south edge of the stand of oak.

To the west the sun had dropped well below the horizon and to the east a passing cloud for the moment had blocked out the glow of the rising moon. Darkness had once again settled upon the prairie and with it came the uncertainty and quietness of the night. Still Bear stood, his ear turned to the wind and his eyes searching the darkness, and even though he was unable to see no more than ten feet in front of him, he knew soon the cloud would be gone and the moon's soft glow would once again light the clearing, hopefully giving him enough light to see anything as big as a man trying to approach. It would be that way until another cloud came drifting by. "I don't understand," he mumbled to himself in a low voice. Then he thought, those were some fine folks, honest, hardworking people. *They had no money or nothing else of any real value that I know of, and I doubt if whoever did this got more than ten dollars total. Ten dollars, now that's not much of a windfall for the taking of three innocent lives.* Suddenly hearing the rustling of leaves, he spun around, looking in the direction of approaching footsteps.

"Supper's ready," Zack said walking up.

After supper, they shook out their bedrolls and with Mushy taking first watch, the other two men crawled in. But sleep did not come easily for Bear Townsend, for no matter how hard he tried, he could not seem to shake

Showdown at Deer Creek

the thought of the Penningtons or how they had died. Realizing he was not going to be able to sleep anyway, he thought it only right to change out with Mushy, which he did. When the sun came up the next morning, the old bull of the herd was still standing watch.

While the coffee brewed, Zack and Mushy saddled the horses and made their way back to the fire where Bear had poured each a cup. "I don't know," he began as the two men walked up. "If it's been two weeks like Zack said, it might be awful hard to pick up the trail. You know that whole place is nothing but rock, and more rock. How Bill and Bernice ever got that vegetable garden to grow I'll never know, but they did and a nice one, too."

"We'll find it," Mushy broke in. "If not, we'll just head south toward Mexico. That's bound to be where they're headed. I know if I'd done something like this that's for sure the trail I'd be riding."

"Yeah, but you're a reasonable man, Uncle Mushy," Zack replied. "We're not dealing with reasonable men here. We're dealing with cold blooded killers, men who have no respect for life or the law, and they sure don't think like you and me or Pa there."

"We'll know more once we get there and have a look around," Bear cut in. Standing, he kicked dirt on the fire, then flipping the last few drops of coffee from the cup he said, "drink up boys. It's time to be making dust."

It was late morning when they drew up on the little rise west of the Pennington house. Their presence didn't go unnoticed long, for Bear had not had time to adjust himself in the saddle before Butler Van Dill stood from behind cover and taking off his hat, waved it high above his head signaling them to ride on in.

Bear nudged his horse on, but it wasn't until he turned north and started across the yard did he notice that there were three crudely made crosses marking three freshly dug graves on the south side of the old barn. It was then he realized Bill Pennington and his family were truly gone. "Why, oh why," he mumbled as he rode. Then he looked down and seeing the dark, blood-stained ground where Bill had lay and bled out, a cold shiver ran up his spine. He tried desperately to speak, to say something, but the words would not come. The awful lump in his throat had stopped them so and he just sat quietly with his hands resting on the pommel.

"Mornin' Bear," Mavis said with a nod, then throwing up a hand in the direction of the graves he added, "got 'em took care of, we found an old tarp out there in the barn and wraped 'em in it, and buried 'em deep."

"Sure did," Teal agreed. "Buried 'em good and deep, and believe me, it ain't no easy job diggin' in this here rock, and we wouldn't have ever got it done either if we hadn't found those two long-handled picks there in the barn."

"Except we ain't said no words over 'em yet," Mavis interrupted. "We found a Good Book there in the house, but can't neary one of us read a word. Kinda figured you'd know some proper words to say."

"I'm obliged," Bear said with a nod to each. Then

stepping to the ground, he threw his reins over the hitch rail and started up the steps, but when he reached for the door handle, a strange feeling came over him and he suddenly stopped. He stood for a long moment staring down at the handle, then turning, he walked from the porch in the direction of the graves, and as he made his way across the hard-packed, grassless, rocky ground the other men slowly followed along behind.

"Made 'em some markers," Butler said, "got their names out of the Good Book there in the house, burnt 'em in with a piece of hot wire."

"I see that," Bear answered. "You boys did a mighty fine job and I'm more than sure old Bill would appreciate all you've done." Then reaching up, he slowly removed his hat and after a short pause to think he said, "Lord, there's really not a whole lot I can say about these fine people you don't already know. They were good, honest, hardworking folks with no enemies I know of and our lives won't be the same without 'em. So I'm just going to leave it at that. Amen." Then looking over at the other men he said, "if no one's got anything else to add, there's nothing left for us to do here but get on our horses and see if we can pick up the trail that will lead us to the men who are responsible." Then crossing back to his horse, Bear took up his reins and after taking another long, hard look in the direction of the three graves, he stepped into leather and when all the men had gathered around he said, "men, we want to split up in two's and ride in a tight circle around this place and with each pass, we'll make the circle a little wider then a little wider. You're going to have to look at the ground closely, boys, to find anything and let me tell you right now, what you find won't be much because it's been two weeks or longer. As you can see, it's almost solid rock, but it might be just enough to get us headed in the right direction." With that said, Bear pointed, "Butler, you go with Zack, Teal with Mushy, and Mavis you can stay with me." Then adjusting himself in the saddle, he touched his horse with a spur and moved out.

Bear knew, as did the rest of the men, the house had been built in a little grassy flat where there was only shallow soil, and for some distance in either direction around the house there was nothing but rocks, big rocks. It was in one of those rocks that over the years a crack had somehow formed, and through that crack water from down deep flowed up to create the spring. But it was somewhere among those same large rocks that he or one of the others would have to find the first clue, a scuff mark left behind by a sliding horse hoof, or the remains of a discarded cigarette, or drop of blood, or even where someone had spat tobacco. It was finding such a clue that would hopefully lead to another and then another until the direction the killers had rode out would be clear.

By evening, the circle had widened to the third pass and the hopes of finding the trail before having to head back to the Pennington house for the night was quickly fading. The sun hung low in the western sky, and even though it was still well above the thin line of dark

Showdown at Deer Creek   131

clouds that had gathered along the horizon, it seemed to be dropping fast. Hearing horse hooves clicking against rock, Bear looked in that direction to see Mushy and Teal coming along the trail.

"Found where they crossed a dry creek bottom back south aways," Mushy said as he drew up.

"Then they're headed south," Bear replied. "You said they'd head for Mexico."

"No, sir. They were coming north, Bear, and from the looks of the tracks, I'd say there's at least five of 'em. Me and Teal rode the creek out in both directions for a good ways and never did find where they'd crossed it going back south."

"Well," Bear started, then taking a deep, ragged breath and letting it out slowly he said, "we might as well call it a day. It'll be dark before we get back to the house as it is." But he had no more than said those words when they heard Zack call out.

"Maybe they've found something," Mushy said as he put a hard spur to his horse, and by the time they had ridden to within sight, Zack was squatted on his heels almost dead center of a boulder some twenty feet across and he had his eyes turned to the ground.

"Found me a shod track," he said, "and it's a good one, too. As clear as it was just made this morning."

Bear quickly slid from his horse to have a closer look and sure enough there was a small indention in the rock and in that indention enough blowing sand had gathered that when the horse's hoof came down it, he left a track. Instantly a big smile came to his lips and he said, "ok, you men, spread out. If we found one, maybe we can find another."

With all six men looking in the same area, it didn't take long for someone to find a scuff mark, then another, and a little later another track, but by the time they had worked their way clear of the rocks out onto the prairie where there was softer ground and where the tracking would be somewhat easier, it was getting late. But Bear had seen enough to know the men they sought were headed west northwest and upon realizing their direction he said, "if they don't change directions on us, Mushy, they're headed straight for the panhandle, maybe up to Colorado."

"I don't know why anyone would want to go there," Mushy answered. "I'm kinda looking for 'em to change, Bear. I'm figuring they'll turn west somewhere before long and head into the Bad Lands. Ain't no water in the panhandle, ain't no whole lot of nothing but a bunch of scalp takin' Indians."

Because of his younger eyes and the dimming light, Zack had taken over the lead but before long he too would have to give up, for late evening was upon them and soon it would be too dark to see the ground from atop a horse, much less a track or a bent blade of grass. Then all of a sudden, he swung his horse east and rode off in that direction for quite aways.

Bear raised his hand, bringing the men to a stop and sat watching as his son read the sign.

Zack rode at a canter to the top of the next little rise where he drew up and stepped to the ground and walked along for a good bit tailing his reins.

Showdown at Deer Creek

"I don't have a good feeling 'bout him ridin' from the trail like that," Bear said, looking over at Mushy.

But before Mushy could answer, Zack took off his hat and swinging it high above his head waved them over.

"They've turned on us," he said as the men rode up. "They're headed east."

"Deer Creek," Bear blurted, "they're headed for Deer Creek."

"We don't know where they're going," Mushy replied, "and it's not looking much like they do either. We'll just have to stay with the trail and see."

"You're right, Mushy, they may change directions again, before this deal is done, they may be in Mexico like you said this morning. But it's getting too late to see anything now so we might as well make camp. We'll get back after 'em in the morning." He led the way to a little grove of trees where they were not long in starting supper and a pot of coffee, but still down deep in the pit of his stomach Bear Townsend had an awful feeling, a feeling the trail they were now on would somehow lead to Deer Creek, and if she hadn't left for home, Deer Creek was where Becky was getting fitted for her new wedding dress.

Chapter Six

The silver dollar hit the table with a loud, distinctive ring. "I call," Truitt said without looking up from the five cards in his hand.

"Ok, let me see 'em," Blackie replied.

Truitt slowly fanned the cards and laid them on the table. "Not much, just a pair of tens, but since you drew three, I thought I'd give it a shot."

Blackie smiled. "Not bad thinking for an outlaw." Then giving his head an easy shake, he added, "I wish I had better news for you, Truitt, but a pair of tens ain't going to get the job done." Then slowly flipping his cards one at a time face up on the table he said with a big hoot 'n holler, "read 'em and weep *amigo*. I've got you beat two ways, so I'll let you take your pick, a pair of jacks or three sevens." He gave a loud, roaring belly laugh and slapped hard at the table. "I was sittin' here holding a full house, sevens over jacks." Reaching over, he dragged the money toward him and as he did, Truitt pushed up to his feet.

"Hey, where you going?" Blackie asked. "It's still early yet."

"That's it, I've had enough," Truitt answered. "I'm finished, Blackie, you've done cleaned me out." Picking up the half empty glass from the table, he tossed down the last of the whiskey. Then turning an eye back to Blackie he added, "I think I'll go have a look around town, kinda give my legs a stretch."

"If you happen to see R.C.," Blackie said, "tell 'im we need to get all these do-gooders rounded up, it's gettin' dark." Just then the batwing doors swung open and he looked up. "Just the man I wanted to see," Blackie said in a loud voice. "It's fixin' to be dark, R.C., so I'm a-figgerin' we better roundup all these fine do-gooders and get 'em to where we can keep an eye on 'em."

"Got the men already doin' just that," R.C. answered as he slowly removed his hat. "Hank and Bull anyway. Tatum's still up in the loft of the livery stable with his eyes on the east trail. He's sure got his head set on killin' somebody, be it today, tomorrow or the next day, but sooner or later he's going to kill somebody."

"He better not kill that sheriff," Blackie said abruptly, "he's mine. I'll take care of him myself, but the loft is a good place for 'im the way he's been acting and all, he's just about to get on my bad side. That girl over there has really got his mind rattled, not that Stillwell has a whole lot of mind to start with, but what little bit he does have she's for sure got it rattled."

"You think her pa will really pay to get her back?" R.C. asked.

"Yes, I do. Just look at her sittin' over there," Blackie said pointing. "She's been bought educated, and look at the shine in her hair, the softness of her skin and her clothes. She came from money, R.C., big money, and I'm aimin' to have even more of her old man's money when this deal is done than I do now, a lot more." He gave his shoulders a shrug then added, "if I'm wrong and he don't want to pay, well then, we'll just see how he likes burying his little girl after Stillwell gets finished with her. He offered me his part of the bank for her, so I'm not going to lose out either way."

"What if her pappy don't show up at all?" R.C. asked. "What are we going to do then?"

"Oh, he'll show alright, you can count on that," Blackie answered with confidence. "But if he don't, we'll just have to ride by his place and have a little talk with 'im on our way out of town. It looks to me like we're goin' to have to ride out by there anyway to find that other loudmouth, that Mushy fellow."

"I wish the sheriff would hurry up and get back," R.C. cut in, "so you can kill 'im and we can be clear of this place. It's startin' to get on my nerves."

"Mine too. He'll be coming along," Blackie answered. "And believe me when he does show, he's going wish he'd stayed in Fort Worth by the time I'm finished with 'im."

Becky had clearly overheard the conversation between the two outlaws and knew time was slowly but surely running out, that sooner or later her pa or Lane were bound to show up and when they did, someone was going to die. She quickly glanced over at Sam who sat at the table across from her, but before she could say anything, the batwing doors pushed open and the towns folk started through. Mr. and Mrs. Scott were leading the way and Mr. Scott was sporting a new bandage around his badly injured head. Behind them walked Edith McNare, then Mrs. Mahony and her two kids, and they were followed by another twenty-five or so people, all of whom Becky knew and knew well. They all looked so tired, and beat, and frightened, and many seemed to be laboring just to move their feet and none walked with their heads up. Becky sat in total horror as the fine people of Deer Creek, people she had known all her life were driven like cattle toward the back of the saloon, people too afraid to speak, and afraid to cast their eyes in any direction but down.

"Why don't you just let us go home?" Mr. Scott asked, turning to Blackie. "I give you my word we won't try anything. I promise."

"Now wouldn't that be nice," Blackie answered with a smirk. "I just bet you do wish I'd let you go home. No, y'all are going to stay right here until I say otherwise. Now get on back yonder and I don't want to hear another word out of you or anyone else or you'll get some more of what I gave you before, and that would be a shame for me to have to mess up that nice, clean, white bandage."

"Leave 'im alone," Mrs. Scott yelled at Blackie. "Haven't you people done enough? You almost killed him and now you've taken the money from his bank, what more do you people want?"

Blackie's eyes narrowed as he stepped toward the old lady and as he did, he reached down for his gun. "Some people don't ever learn," he said, and as he got within reach, he swung the gun at her head.

George Scott threw up his right arm to block the blow coming at his wife and with his left he took a wild, half-hearted swing in Blackie's direction, catching the killer with only a glancing blow to the side of his head. But it was enough to send an instant wave of mad, killing rage through the outlaw, and the shot that followed sent a sudden loud gasp over the crowd of onlookers.

The old man's body flinched with the impact of the bullet and at the same instant, he grabbed at the pain in his stomach with his right hand, and reached for the bar with his left, his face went blank to the world and his mouth closed tight as the pain grew. He stood straight on stiff legs for a long moment as though nothing was wrong, then he began staggering ever so slowly backwards and as he did, his eyes locked on the man who had shot him and he mumbled, "you've killed me, sir." His body began to sway first one way then the other and then his knees buckled and as life slipped away, he crumbled slowly to the floor.

"George!" Mrs. Scott called out as she dropped to the floor beside her husband. "Please, George," she cried, "oh, please, George. Please don't go—George—George, please don't go."

Blackie stood over the Scotts with his six-gun still smoking in his hand, then thumbing the hammer back,

Showdown at Deer Creek 139

he pointed it at the side of Mrs. Scott's head and just as he started to pull the trigger Sam jumped to his feet, "what are you going to shoot her for?" he screamed out.

Blackie spun at the sudden loud voice and pulled the trigger, letting a bullet fly that struck Sam high on the left shoulder. The back of Sam's shirt puffed out when the bullet made its exit and bright red blood splatter on the nearby wall. The impact sent the big man spinning, then crashing through a table, and as he landed flat of his back on the floor, he let out a loud painful groan. Blackie fanned another quick shot in his direction that struck the floor just inches from Sam's head, sending splinters high in the air.

Blackie's eyes flashed red and his face grew dark as he started in Sam's direction. Getting to him, he reached down and got Sam by the hair and yanked his head up and as he did, he shoved the muzzle of the pistol right up against his forehead and said, "that's been your problem all along, Mr. Saddle Maker, worryin' too much about other people, and not enough about yourself."

Thinking for sure Blackie was going to shoot Sam again, Becky started to stand in hopes of rushing the outlaw and somehow getting his gun, but a hand suddenly on her shoulder forced her back down hard into the chair. She turned to see R.C. standing behind her with his gun drawn. "You may want to think 'bout maybe just sittin' there and not sayin' nothin'," he said, "this could get a mite ugly."

"Give me one good reason why I shouldn't blow

your fool head off right now!" Blackie yelled. But before Sam could say anything, the outlaw forced Sam's head hard against the floor, then raising the injured man's head again, he slammed it down against the floor a second time.

"He needs a doctor," Becky screamed out.

"The only doctorin' he's goin' to get, if he gets any at all, is what you can give him," Blackie said to Becky. "Now, if you want to, get over here and see 'bout 'im, but if you don't, let 'im lay there. But let me warn you, and let this be a warning to all of you fine do-gooders," he shouted while taking a long, hard look at the rest of the captives, "I'm only goin' to say it one more time. If you don't do what I say when I say, I'm goin' to kill you. I'm goin' to kill every last one of you. I don't know how many times I'm goin' to have to say something before you people start believing me." Then he slowly motioned to the dead man with his gun barrel and said, "Bull, you and Hank get 'im on over to the livery stable and put 'im with the rest of 'em."

"Don't touch him," Mrs. Scott cried out as the two outlaws approached. "Don't you dare touch him." Looking at Blackie through red, tearstained eyes she said in a shaky voice, "I hope you're happy with yourself. Now look at what you've done. You've killed him, you've killed a good man for no reason. George Scott was a fine, dear, decent man, and twice the man you'll ever think about being, in life or in death."

"I killed him?" Blackie sneered. "I didn't kill 'im. You killed 'im by running that smart mouth of yours."

Mrs. Scott wiped at the tears, then the snot running

from her nose with a sleeve and said, "I hope you rot in hell for what you've done here today."

"Somebody better get this old hag up and back yonder out of my way." Blackie yelled. "Her smart mouth is startin' to make me mad, and y'all don't want to see me when I'm mad. No, you sure don't."

Reaching over, Mrs. Mahony took Mrs. Scott by the arm and helped her to her feet, and then leading the way toward the back, they found a chair where the sobbing Mrs. Scott reluctantly took a seat.

"R.C., on second thought," Blackie screamed out, "take all these fine folks and put 'em in the hotel. I'm tired of all their whining. Leave the girl, the cook, and the saddle maker here, but get the rest of 'em out of my sight."

"The bullet went all the way through," Becky said to Sam who was still lying on the floor. Taking a red-checkered tablecloth from a nearby table, she quickly tore it into strips and started gently cleaning, then wrapping the wound.

Darkness had once again fallen upon the little town, and an awful, eerie quietness had filled the saloon. The only sounds being made was the jingle of Blackie Getts spurs as he nervously paced back and forth from the bar to the table by the window, and an occasional low, painful groan from Sam as Becky did her best to stop the flow of blood. Again the towns folk would settle in for another long, fearful night of wonder and uncertainty that the darkness seemed to bring, but all knew their future, if there was such a thing, would not be the same, for George Scott had just been killed. Shot dead right before their very eyes by the heartless, murderer Blackie Getts. Though no one spoke a word as they left the saloon, it was evident by the blank look on all their faces they were wondering who next would say or do some little something that would cost them their lives.

"There you go, Sam," Becky said getting to her feet. "That's the best I can do. You're lucky it hit so high up, but I bet that muscle is going to be plenty sore by morning."

Sam gave a slow, thankful nod and replied, "you did a mighty fine job patchin' me up, Becky. But I don't have to wait til morning 'cause it's already hurtin' like all get out, but by you takin' care of it quick like you did, I'll be as good as new in a couple of days."

"Do you really think we're still going to be alive in a couple of days, Sam?" Becky asked. "They've already killed what, four, no, five people, and it would have been six but you stopped Getts from killing Mrs. Scott. And you're only alive because the bullet went high and the other missed your head or you'd be dead right now and number seven."

Sam looked up at Becky, his eyes blood-shot from the pain. "I know," he said in a low whisper. "They're going to kill us all. We've done overheard 'em saying they were, but right now there's nothing we can do and anything we attempt will only get someone else killed. There's just too many of 'em, Becky. No, our only chance is for your pa to show up with some of his men or for Lane to figger out what's going on before he rides in here. That way maybe he can ride out to the Running T and get some help. He can't do it by himself and neither can we. What we need to do is try to keep Blackie and that bunch calm, do what they say, when they say. Surely Bear or Lane one will show up around here tomorrow or the next day. For all we know they may be out there right now waitin' in the darkness somewhere for the right time to ride in."

"I didn't say y'all could talk," Blackie called out. "I said you could patch 'im up if you wanted to, but no talking." After a pause he added, "Little Missy, when you get finished with whatever it is you're doing there, get a rag or mop and clean up that blood there on the floor."

"If you'd just stop shootin' people," Becky snapped, "there wouldn't be any blood on the floor to clean up." But remembering what Sam had just said about keeping the outlaws calm and doing what they said she looked over at Blackie and said in a much kinder voice, "ok—ok, Blackie, I'll get it cleaned up."

Blackie looked quickly at Hank and half laughing said, "by heavens, I think she's finally gettin' the hang of it."

Becky extended her hand, "Here," she said to Sam, "take hold and I'll help you over to that chair yonder."

After Sam was back on his feet, Becky put another strip of the tablecloth around his neck and made a sling for his arm. Then after getting him settled in the chair, she let her eyes search the room for a mop, but unable to see one, she took another red-checkered tablecloth from a table and started wiping up the blood. Hearing footsteps, she looked up to see Blackie coming toward her with a bottle in his hand and when he got to where she knelt, he said, "no water. Here, maybe this will help."

Turning up the bottle he poured a good amount of the whiskey onto the floor, then as slowly as he had come, he turned and started back toward the table by the window.

Becky watched him go and when the killer had dropped back in the chair, she started slowly doing what she'd been ordered to do. She worked the whiskey well into the wood and as she did the blood lifted. Then with a final swipe of the tablecloth the red stain for the most part was gone. But as she started to stand she got an awful, uncomfortable feeling. It was the same feeling she'd been trying desperately to resist for the last hour or so, the feeling of needing to make a trip to the outhouse. But with the discomfort now growing more prevalent she knew it was only a matter of time, before she would be forced to ask for permission. That meant one of the outlaws would be ordered to go with her and stand guard at the door while she was inside. But somehow managing to suppress the urge one more time, she made her way back to the table and took a seat, but only moments passed before the discomfort came again. Knowing there was not but one thing she could do, she got to her feet and started in the direction of the table where Blackie sat.

He looked up from his drink as she approached. "What can I do for you Little Missy?"

Her face flushed red with embarrassment. "I need to go out back," she answered in a whisper.

"Out back," he echoed in a loud voice, "Can't you wait till morning?" But before Becky could answer, he said, "you're gettin' to be more trouble than you're worth, girl." Looking across the table, Blackie jerked his head toward the back door and said, "Hank, you go this time."

Becky was glad Blackie had chosen Hank because for the most part he didn't seem to be as bad as the rest. And when he spoke his voice was soft and low and at times even polite, and the taking of human life didn't seem to always be first on his mind. But she knew, as they all did, that for him to ride with the likes of Blackie Getts, he had to be a killer and to even think about taking him lightly would be a bad mistake, and more apt than not, probably a fatal one.

Out on the porch, Becky stopped and stood for a moment staring through the darkness in the direction of the outhouse. The lanterns Red kept hung here and there in trees along the path to light the way were not lit as they normally would be, and though the moon hung high and bright in the night sky, it was so dark under the canopy of oak she could barely see her hand passing in front of her face. Turning to the outlaw she asked, "are you going to light the lanterns?"

"Blackie didn't say nothin' 'bout lightin' no lanterns," Hank replied dryly. "So I don't figger I'll be lightin' any."

"Maybe he just forgot," Becky said. "I'm sure he'd want 'em lit."

"Well, he might," Hank said after thinking, "and I don't reckon it would hurt nothin' to maybe fire up just one or two. That for sure would help a person see a little better, and like you say, it is purty dark. There could be an old rattler laying here somewhere just awaitin' to take a bite." After another long moment of what seemed to be serious thinking on the outlaw's part, he gently nudged Becky on down the steps and as they came to a lantern, he lit it and then another and as the flames took life, the pathway emerged from the darkness and then the little unpainted, slatboard building.

With no time to spare, Becky entered the little building, quickly latching the bolt behind her. A short time later, and just as she was getting ready to leave, she heard a loud thud, and almost instantly a low groan, followed by the sound of what she thought to be a person falling to the ground. "Hank?" she called out through the door. "Are you there?" But she got no reply. "Hank?" she called out again. "Are you ok?" But like before she got no reply. Suddenly a faint smile came to her lips and she called out in a low voice, "Lane, is that you?" But like the other times, she got no reply. She held her breath and turned an ear trying to hear but the only sounds being made were of the frogs croaking along the creek to the south, and from high in the tree just outside, the broken hoot from an old owl. I wonder what's going on out there, she thought to herself. Had Hank somehow stumbled over something in the dark and fell and maybe struck his head and knocked himself out? If so, now would be a good time to take his gun, or maybe he's just went back inside for some reason. "No that couldn't be it," she answered herself in a low voice. "Blackie would have his hide for leaving me unguarded." She pressed her ear tight against the door trying her best to hear, but she heard nothing. Then reaching over, she slowly unlatched the bolt and ever so cautiously pushed the door open to just a crack. Looking through with one eye, she searched the darkness as far as she could see but saw nothing, then opening the door just a little further, she got a better look but still saw nothing. She stood perfectly still, trying to listen, but this time heard only the frogs. The old owl must have flown away or maybe he was sitting on a high up limb watching in silence. She gave the door another little push, giving her only enough room to stick her head out, but just as she did, she saw a sudden sweeping dark shadow coming at her and before she could duck, a fist caught her solidly in the mouth, snapping her head back hard. A sudden sharp pain rushed through her mouth and head and at the same instant, her knees went weak. She felt the warm blood as it gushed from her badly busted lips and ran down to her chin. She grabbed frantically for the door, or wall, or anything that would stop her fall but it was not to be, and with consciousness quickly slipping away, she crumbled to the floor. The door swung open and as it did, she rubbed at her eyes with a weak, uncontrolled hand, trying to clear them of the awful blur and saw only the shadow of a man standing there and as her consciousness drifted deeper and deeper into darkness, she realized the man's dim outline showed he was wearing a derby hat.

"Hank!" Blackie called out. Then grabbing the unconscious man by the shirt, he raised him slightly from the ground, and gave him a good solid slap to his face and then a hard shake. "Hank, what happened? Where's the girl?"

"Here," R.C. said, "maybe this will bring 'im

around. Reaching over Blackie's left shoulder, he dumped a half bottle of whiskey into the man's face.

Hank gasped hard for air as he came up to a sitting position, then instantly rubbed at his burning eyes, trying to clear them of the stinging liquid. "What's going on here?" he asked in a slurred, somewhat mumbling voice.

"You tell me," Blackie said. "What happened? Where's the girl?"

Hank reached for the pain in the back of his head. "I don't rightly know, Blackie. Somebody hit me from behind. I didn't see anything."

"It's got to be that sheriff," Blackie yelled, turning to R.C. he said, "get the men. Those two have got to be here somewhere and we're going to find 'em." Turning back, he asked the man on the ground, "can you watch after those do-gooders in there?"

Hank gave his throbbing head a slow, easy nod. "Yeah, I can watch 'em. I'm alright, Blackie, just a little fuzzy-headed, that's all. Whoever it was that hit me was sure trying to knock my head off."

Blackie helped Hank up to his feet, then reaching down, he picked up his hat and after giving it a good hard dusting against his leg, he handed it over and said, "you get back in there and keep an eye on 'em, and if any, and I mean any of 'em as much as blinks their eyes the wrong way, you shoot 'em, and you shoot 'em good and dead."

Hank gave a nod, then slowly eased his hat onto his sore, throbbing head, but as he turned toward the back

Showdown at Deer Creek

door, he saw R.C. and Bull coming out. "We've got trouble," R.C. said as he made his way down the steps.

"What are you talking about?" Blackie asked. But noticing they were a man short he asked, "where's Stillwell?"

"That's the trouble," R.C. replied. "He's not at the livery stable. I don't know where he is."

Blackie reached up and pushed his hat back, then rubbed worriedly at his beard. "I told 'im—I told 'im if he messed with that girl I'd kill 'im, and he can't say I didn't, 'cause y'all all heard me tell 'im."

"You don't know it was Tatum that hit Hank," R.C. replied.

"Do you want to bet me a hundred it wasn't?" Blackie asked. "If it wasn't him then where's he at? Why ain't he up in the loft at the livery stable where he's supposed to be?"

"I don't know, Blackie," R.C. answered, "but that sheriff might have got 'im. Who knows, he may be lying around here dead somewhere."

"By the time I'm finished with 'im he's going to wish the sheriff had got 'im alright, and you can count on 'im being dead. Now you boys spread out, take each building and look 'em over good. If Tatum's got that girl, we don't have much time. We may already be too late."

"You want me to give you a hand lookin' for 'em?" Truitt asked from the porch.

Blackie paused for a moment to think. In his own mind he knew Stillwell, and not the sheriff had taken the girl and if he in fact was the one, Blackie knew he was going to have to kill him for doing it. He had told him flat-out in front of all the men on at least two different occasions that he couldn't have her, and that she wasn't for sale, and for him to leave her alone. So if Tatum was the one, he couldn't just let him get by with disobeying an order. How would something like that look to the rest of the men? They may all get to thinking they could do whatever they wanted whenever they wanted to. No, as much as he liked Tatum, and as much as he needed him, and even though the girl was probably going to die anyway, he couldn't have one of his men disobeying an order. Looking up at Truitt he said, "yeah, you better give us a hand."

Sam sat watching the back door and when he noticed Hank walk through by himself, a sudden wave of fear washed over him and he instantly pushed up from the table. "What's wrong?" he asked worriedly. Then looking past the outlaw and not seeing his good friend, he asked. "Where's Becky? Why ain't she with you? What's all the loud talk about out there?"

"Sit down and shut up," Hank replied bitterly. "If Blackie catches you talking it's not going to set well with 'im, and from the looks of your arm there, you should take his advice and worry more 'bout yourself and less about others."

"Where's Becky?" Sam demanded. "What have you people done with her?"

At the man's loud, defiant words, Hank's eyes flashed fire and his face grew dark as he started across the room in Sam's direction, and as he did, he dropped his hand down for his six-gun. "I said sit down and shut your mouth, and if you know what's good for you, you'll do it right now."

Hoping to stop or to at least lessen the assault he saw coming, Sam dropped back to the chair, and as the outlaw got to within reach, he threw up his one good arm to block the blow.

Hank started a wide, sweeping swing with the gun, but for some reason, suddenly stopped and just stood looking down into the defeated eyes of Sam Stovall. Without saying a word, the outlaw slowly holstered the gun, then turning, he started back across the floor in the direction of the table by the window. But as he walked away, Sam noticed that Hank's shirt was soaked to the waist and there was a strong smell of whiskey, then he noticed the bright red blood along the shirt's collar and on the back of Hank's head.

I wonder what happened to him, Sam thought. Had Becky somehow got the better of this man and made her escape to freedom? Or had Lane or maybe Bear made their way into town under the cover of darkness and took Hank Hardin by surprise, hitting him with something hard enough to leave one terrible gash and a lump the size of a hen egg on the back of his head? Was help finally on the way? Or was that just wishful thinking, or was it something else altogether. Maybe Becky had tried to overpower Hank in an attempt to get away and had somehow got hurt or worse yet, killed. To these awful questions he had no real answers, and it didn't look as though he would be getting any from Hank or anyone else. All he knew for sure was when Becky walked out of the saloon, Hank was with her and when he came back, he was by himself and the back of his head and shirt were covered in blood. Where was Blackie Getts? Sam knew that over the past four days it was not unusual for Bull, Hank, Tatum or even R.C. to be away from the saloon for hours on end, but it was highly unusual for Blackie to be gone for more than fifteen or twenty minutes at a time. Then Sam remembered R.C. had come through the back door and mysteriously called Blackie out some time ago, and Blackie had not been seen since. Hearing footsteps on the boardwalk, Sam swung his eyes toward the batwing doors just as R.C. pushed through.

"Where's Blackie?" R.C. asked.

"Still out back I reckon," Hank answered, throwing up a hand in that direction.

Without speaking again, R.C. moved quickly across the room and out the back door, but not finding his boss within the dim glow of the lanterns, he called out into the darkness, "Blackie."

"Over here," a voice called back.

R.C. made his way toward the voice and when he had found him he said, "it's Tatum alright, or at least I figger it is. I checked the livery stable again and he's for sure not there."

Blackie took a long, hard, ragged, disgusted breath and as he let it out, he said, "I'd already figgered that much." After a short pause, he added, "let's go see if we can find 'im. R.C., you take Bull and you two work the north side of the street and me and Truitt will take the south side, but if'n you find 'im, don't kill 'im. Bring 'im to me."

Showdown at Deer Creek

The four men took the lanterns from along the path and made their way to the front of the saloon where they split up and started along the dark street. Blackie worked his way slowly along the boardwalk, his eyes watching and his ears keen to any sound. In front of the land office he thought for sure he heard sound coming from inside so he drew up to listen. The door squeaked loudly as he slowly pushed it open and stepped through. Instantly, the room filled with the flickering glow from the lantern, but after giving the building a good search, he found nothing. Making his way back out onto the boardwalk, he looked north to see R. C. coming out of the saddle shop. R. C. threw up a hand, giving the all clear sign. Just a little ways on down the street, light shown from the windows of the general store as Bull searched it, and Truitt was just coming out of the dress shop. Blackie rubbed at his beard with a rough hand, "where could he be?" he asked himself in a low voice. Then he remembered seeing a little, freshly painted, brown, slatboard building right at the edge of town the evening he rode in. He had not paid much attention to it because it was getting late, but it was a schoolhouse or something, maybe even a church. "That's where he's at," Blackie mumbled with confidence to himself. Waving Truitt over he said, "I know where to find 'im. Let's go."

The two men hurriedly made their way along the boardwalk, and as they did, shadows grew long and shapeless along the walls of the buildings as the lanterns swung back and forth in their hands. Coming to the last building on the west end, they stepped from the boardwalk and continued on knowing the little brown building was another fifty or sixty yards further west. The moon shined bright from above and its soft glow lit the way, but still the lanterns would be needed because soon they would reach a grove of oak that grew thick and tall, and it was in among those massive old trees the little building had been built and it was there under that giant canopy of branches and leaves that the moonlight would not be able to penetrate. They walked on. Then coming upon a well-traveled path that led off through the oak, they stepped onto it and continued on, but as they walked deeper and deeper into the darkness, the glow of the lanterns became much brighter and more shadows danced. Suddenly, Blackie drew up and instantly squatted on his heels beside a tree. "Just as I figgered," he said in a low voice, as he pointed to light coming from a not too distant window. Then turning to Truitt he said, "we better blow out these lanterns. We don't want 'im seein' us before we see him."

With the lanterns out they sat them down and started on along the path, but now they moved through the darkness slow and hunkered down. The path lead right up to the porch of the little one room schoolhouse. There Blackie turned to Truitt and took a finger up to his lips for quiet. Being ever so careful not to make any noise, he slowly made his way up the steps, then moving one foot at a time, crossed to the door. There he paused for a moment to listen to the voice coming from inside and as he realized it was Tatum doing the talking, his fist clenched white, and a hot wave of anger washed over him, but not ready to open the door just

Showdown at Deer Creek

yet, he removed his hat and slowly eased his head to where he could see through a small gap between the bottom of the curtains and the windowsill. He saw Becky lying flat on her back on a big wooden desk near the blackboard. She was obviously unconscious or maybe even already dead and Tatum sat in a chair beside her holding her hand and slowly stroking her long, red hair. He was speaking as though she could hear what he was saying but from what Blackie could see, Tatum's words were falling on unconscious ears.

"I didn't mean to hit you so hard," Tatum said in a shaky, half sobbing voice. "I knew you were going to scream out so I was just trying to keep you quiet. I love you, Becky and I want to take you away from here, away from this hard land. Back east to a place where you can dress in nice clothes and eat fine food, a place where we can begin a new life, a place where we can maybe start a family." He reached deep inside his shirt and pulled out the money from the bank. "Look Becky," he said. "I've got money, a lot of money and it's all ours."

Over the past couple of minutes it had become apparent to Blackie that Stillwell had lost a good part of his wit. He was talking like a crazy man, talking like Becky Townsend might someday care for him. It was obvious by the girl's lack of response and movement that it was a one-sided conversation and she was more than likely already dead. Blackie reached down and slipped the leather thong from over the hammer of his pistol and loosened it in the holster. Then taking a quick step back, he let a foot fly and with a loud crash, the door ripped from its hinges.

Tatum Stillwell looked in the direction of the loud crash and when he saw Blackie enter his pulse quickened. Blackie came to a stop just inside the door, then brushing his coattail back, he positioned his hand over the butt of his six-gun. "You poor crazy fool," he said as he started his draw. At the same instant, Tatum reached down for his gun and as he did, his body flinched trying to move but the loud roar and bright, blue muzzle flash told him he was already too late. The bullet ripped at his skull just above his left eye, forcing the brown derby high into the air, the impact of the bullet snapping his head back with so much force it toppled the chair and Tatum hit the floor, but he was unaware of just how badly he'd been beaten on the draw for he was already dead.

Blackie slowly holstered his pistol and as he did, he turned to Truitt, "you still wantin' to hook up?" he asked. "'Cause if you are, I'm a man short."

"Yes, sir," Truitt answered with a smile.

Blackie gave his head a nod and said, "ok then, from here on out you're ridin' with me. Your first job will be to pick up that money there on the floor and try not to get anymore blood on it than there already is."

"I'll sure be careful, Blackie," Truitt replied. "You can count on that."

At the sound of sudden footsteps on the porch, Blackie quickly turned and dropped his hand to the butt of his six-gun but stopped his draw when he realized it was R. C. and Bull coming through the door. But noticing blood running down Bull's face he asked, "what happened to him?"

"I got tangled up in a couple of lanterns someone left

sittin' on the ground back yonder aways," Bull answered, while mopping at his head with a sleeve. "I fell and hit my head on a tree trunk."

Blackie smiled, then looking at Truitt, he shrugged his shoulders and said, "I wonder who would go and leave lanterns sittin' in the middle of a trail like that?" After taking time to think he added, "R.C., you need to get a wagon and get these bodies on over to the livery."

"Ok," R.C. replied. "But I don't know why you want us to take the girl."

"She's dead," Blackie answered.

"No, she ain't," R.C. replied. "At least not all the way dead, 'cause I just seen her hand move."

Blackie moved over to have a closer look, "well, maybe she ain't, I just saw all the blood and knowing Tatum the way I do, I mean did, I just kinda figgered she was." Bending over, Blackie placed an ear near Becky's nose and mouth and a big smile came to his lips when he heard air. "You're right, R.C., she ain't dead," he happily admitted. "She just got knocked a little silly that's all."

Suddenly Becky let out a low, agonizing moan, and a second later, her eyelids began to quiver, then moments later, they slowly opened. She reached up and rubbed at her head with a shaky hand, but tasting blood, she moved her hand quickly to her badly busted lips and when she touched them, her face flinched and she instantly drew her finger back from the sharp pain. "Who hit me?" she asked.

"No need in you wondering who or why," Blackie answered. "Just be thankful you're still alive." He took her by the arm and pulled her up slowly to a sitting position on the desk and when he stepped aside, she looked down to see a faceless body lying in a pool of blood on the floor. She turned a quick eye in Blackie's direction to ask who it was, but stopped when she noticed the little brown derby hat. Instantly, a cold chill ran through her body, and the words Blackie had last spoken suddenly had meaning. Her lips began to produce a frightened smile but the pain stopped her, but still she smiled and smiled big, but only on the inside, because the man she feared most in life was now dead. He would not hurt her or anyone else ever again. Now, she thought to herself as she slid from the desk. They started with five, then there were six, and now there's only five again. But now that they've killed one of their own, how much longer, a week, a day, an hour, could the good folks of Deer Creek expect to stay alive? Who knows, she thought, we may all be dead by first light. Then she thought, where is Pa and Lane?

Chapter Seven

The moon shined bright from the cloudless sky above, but the trail was dark in among the many oak, mesquite and scattered scrub cedars where they rode, and in places the canyons, gullies and loose rocks made traveling rough. A roughness that could easily cost a horse a broken leg or a man his life with one misplaced hoof. It had been a long and hard ride since leaving the wagon the night before, but now Lane rode in familiar country, country he'd been riding in since he was a boy. And he knew even with good luck, it was still a good day's ride or more to where he needed to be. So he rode on fully aware of the danger but more than willing to take the chance.

"Hey," a voice from behind called out, "if we don't slow up and let these horses rest a mite they're going to quit on us."

Lane drew up and as Tater rode alongside, he rested

his hands on the pommel and answered, "you're right. I must have lost track of the time." Then after taking a moment to think he added, "on up the trail a mile or so there's a seep. If it ain't dry, there'll be water enough for the horses and we can fill our canteens. But if it is, the next water is at Willow Bend another five miles south."

"They're not as thirsty as they are tired and hungry," Tater replied. "We can't keep pushing 'em this way and expect 'em to hold up. We've covered a sight of country in the past few days, hard country. We need to find a place where's there's not only water, but grass. And while I'm thinkin' 'bout it, I could use a cup of coffee myself and maybe even some of those beans I saw you load into your saddlebags."

Lane gave a quick agreeing nod, for like the man talking, he had not had anything to eat since leaving the wagon, and he was god-awful hungry. "I've got to admit that does sound mighty good," he said. Then nudging the horse forward, he rode on leading the way through the night, but as he rode he could not keep from thinking of what Sheriff Moore had said about Blackie Getts. Apparently the law had captured him in the south Texas border town of Presidio after his horse fell during a bank robbery. And they had him locked up tight until his gang rode back in just a few days later and busted him out and in doing so killed the sheriff and both his deputies. And Moore had also said he had sent a wanted poster on Blackie Getts to Deer Creek, but Lane could not remember receiving it, and if he had, he was sure he would have remembered Blackie's badly scarred face. If the man he had in his jail was the same man who escaped, where was his gang? At the time of the shooting and arrest Lane remembered clearly that Getts and the drifter he shot dead were the only two strangers in town. On the other hand if Getts was indeed the man who escaped from the jail down at Presidio, he was a bad sort alright and maybe too bad for an easy going youngster like Tom Walker to handle. But if things got too salty, Walker was fully aware he could call on Sam Stovall, Evret McNare, Lamar Tuggle and even one or two others there in town to give him a hand. And it would not be the first time those men had been called on because Deer Creek had sprang up along the trail leading south to Mexico, and though none were hard men and certainly not gunfighters, over the years they had all dealt with many a man on the run from the law and more than their share of Indians. And all had proven more than once to be men that would hold their ground when needed. And if Lane still found himself needing more help, then there was Bear Townsend, Mushy Crabtree and the rest of the men out at the Running T. Still Lane had that god-awful, uneasy feeling that came upon him from time to time, and it kept gnawing at his insides from down deep in the pit of his stomach. The feeling was of danger and of great urgency. It was the same awful feeling that over the years had proven to be more times right than wrong. It was the feeling of needing to be somewhere he wasn't. And it was for that single reason he rode on, pushing both man and animal well beyond their physical limits, through the darkness, along a trail that was almost too rough for safe travel even in the daylight.

Breaking over the top of a short rise, Lane drew up well within the dark shadows, and as Tater eased alongside, Lane looked over and quickly took a finger to his lips for quiet, then whispered, "we need to go in slow, there may be Indians camped at the seep." Turning back, he stood tall in the stirrups and cast his eyes upon the little moonlit clearing at the bottom. It was some two hundred yards across and all that way there was nothing but grass, not a rock or tree anywhere. He let his eyes move slowly from east to west and knew as he did the giant old oak that marked the seep was another fifty yards or so beyond the distant brush line. It was at the base of that old oak that the cool, clear water seeped up along its roots to form a little pool. But to get there Lane knew they had to cross the clearing and it was crossing that clearing that had him the most worried for the moment because it was while crossing it there would be no cover of any kind, and if there were Indians camped somewhere along the brush on the farside, he and Tater would most likely not ever make it across.

Slowly he let his eyes search the darkness in hopes of maybe spotting a flicker from a campfire, but knew the chances were slim, because Indians were smart and over the years had become second to none when it came to concealing the flames and smoke from a fire. He turned an ear to the wind, but the only sounds were those made by the horses breathing and from the west the lonely cry of a far off nightingale. Other than those few sounds the night was quiet, maybe too quiet. Finally he sniffed the air for the smell of smoke, cooking food, or coffee, but what little breeze there was blew light from the west and he knew if there was someone camped at the seep with a fire, be it white men or Indians, he would never smell it because he was too far north. He knew too, if there was someone camped there they would not be bedded down right at the water's edge but out away from it a good distance in a place where they would hopefully see someone approaching. Turning to Tater he said in a whisper, "when we ride, we want to ride slow, and stay low, and don't stop, and for sure no talking until we're well within the brush on the other side."

Tater without speaking, quickly adjusted himself in the saddle and after pulling his hat down tight he nodded.

Lane gave the clearing one more quick look and listen and when satisfied all was the same as before, he started his horse, and as he did, he leaned forward lying as flat as he could against the pommel and horse's neck.

It wasn't until he made his way from the shadows of the tree-covered rise and had rode well into the moonlit clearing did he notice the movement. Just ahead and a little to the left was something moving slowly through the tall grass, but in the dim moonlight it was still too far away to know for sure what. Lane reached down and slipped the leather thong from over the hammer of his Colt and just as he brought it up, the coyote must have got the scent of a human, because his head shot high above the grass and after giving Lane a short look, he turned and took off fast toward the east, and as the distance quickly grew, his shaggy outline faded into the darkness. "How could I have missed 'im?" Lane asked himself in a low voice, "if that had been an injun he'd be raisin' my scalp 'bout now." He shoved the pistol back into the holster and rode on, but had not gone more than twenty yards or so when all of a sudden a loud flutter came up from the grass. Instantly the horse shied from the unexpected sound at his feet. At the same instant, Lane's pulse quickened, and the sudden side movement by the horse caused him to grab at the pommel to stay on as the unseen covey of quail took wing. Then realizing no Indian would ever miss hearing such a commotion, Lane put a hard spur to the horse and led the way at a full run across the clearing, not reining in until he was well within the dark shadows. There he drew up under the low hanging branches of a giant old oak and as quiet returned, he listened more closely. But it wasn't what he heard that drew his attention first, but what he smelled, and what he smelled was smoke. They had apparently ridden in down wind from a campfire, and the sudden realization made the hair stand stiff on the back of his neck. Looking over at Tater he asked, "you smell it?"

"Smell what?"

"The smoke," Lane replied.

"No. I don't smell any smoke."

"Well I do," Lane answered quietly. "You better have your gun ready 'cause we ain't alone." After a moment

Showdown at Deer Creek

of silence, he added, "we better spread out there's no need in us both gettin' killed with the same bullet." Starting the horse, Lane rode slowly west, picking his way through the dense, tangled brush, and with each step the smell of smoke grew stronger. Coming to a tall, old cottonwood he drew up and sat for a long moment with his ear turned to the wind but not hearing anything, he slowly slid to the ground, then tying his horse to one of the lower limbs, he moved on west through the darkness on foot. All of a sudden the night came alive with what seemed to be undirected gunfire, for none of the bullets struck anywhere close, maybe five or six quick shots in all. Only moments went by before he heard the unmistakable sound of horse hooves pounding rock and hard ground at a gallop, and from the sound, Lane estimated there to be at least two riders. He stood listening as the horses traveled west and did not move until the hoof beats had faded into the far off night. Hearing leaves rusting behind him, he spun with his gun up, but unable to see anything through the darkness, he remained still. Then he heard a low voice say, "don't shoot." Realizing it was Tater, Lane whispered, "that's a good way to get yourself shot."

"What was all the shootin' 'bout?" Tater asked.

"Just someone trying to scare us I reckon."

"Indians?" Tater questioned.

"Not likely," Lane answered, "In the dark, Indians wait for you to come to them, then they kill you without you ever knowing they're there."

"You reckon those that rode off were all of 'em?"

"Maybe, maybe not," Lane answered honestly. "But we won't know for sure till we go have a look." Turning back, Lane started in the direction the smell of smoke was leading him, but he moved slow and with great caution for he knew that just because he didn't think it was Indians didn't mean it wasn't, and he had been wrong before. Furthermore, just because two had apparently ridden off didn't mean there wasn't more waiting somewhere in the darkness for someone to make the mistake of letting their guard down too soon. Coming to a little grassy knoll some twenty yards across and probably twice that distance wide, Lane paused again to listen. The moon's soft glow lit the little knoll and from one side to the other the grass stood tall, green, and lush. Again he sniffed the air and it was evident by the strong presence of smoke he was getting close. But this time what he smelled was somehow different, and it was a smell that made hunger pains stab at his belly, because it was the smell of food cooking. Not wanting to take a chance on someone maybe seeing him crossing the moonlit knoll and taking a shot, Lane turned at right angle and made his way around to the farside staying well within the brush. It was just after pushing his way through a heavy growth of thorny briers did he find what he was looking for. The camp sat in among a small stand of cottonwood, and the fire had been built where the smoke would rise up through the low hanging branches and in doing so break up to disappear from view, but with the light wind the smell of the burning wood lingered. Lane stood letting his ears search the darkness for sound, but after hearing

Showdown at Deer Creek 167

nothing that didn't belong he moved on leading the way toward the smoldering fire.

"Who do you figger it was?" Tater asked.

"I don't know," Lane answered, "but it for sure wasn't injuns."

"How do you know that?"

Lane pointed at the fire. "Indians would have never rode out of here without taking that rabbit there," then he added, "and even though I have seen a few, I've not seen many Indians who drink coffee."

"What makes you think whoever was here was drinking coffee?" Tater asked. "I don't see any pot, and if it was white men, why would they run off and not take the rabbit with 'em?"

"They heard us coming and probably thought we were Indians. Most folks think more of their hair than they do a rabbit. And you're right, Tater, there's no coffee pot," Lane replied, "but look at the rocks surrounding the fire. Those dark stains there are from where whoever it was tried to douse the fire when they heard all the commotion." Lane drew his knife and after testing the rabbit and finding it still needing cooking, he added wood to the fire, and as the flames grew, he looked over at Tater, threw up a pointing hand to the southeast and said, "the seep is over yonder way thirty or so yards. We better gather our horses and after we get 'em to water, we'll hobble 'em on that little grassy knoll we crossed back yonder."

After getting the horses taken care of, the two men made their way back to the fire and while Tater started a pot of coffee, Lane cut the top from a can of beans and poured them into the small pan he had taken from the Olsens' wagon, and with that done, he sat it over the flames to heat.

"You figger the man you've got locked up is the same one the sheriff was talking 'bout?" Tater asked.

Lane looked up surprised, for Tater's question was the very same one Lane had just asked himself. "I don't know," Lane answered in a worried voice. "I sure hope he's not, but from what Sheriff Moore said, he sure might be." Lane paused then asked, "Tater, you were in the cell right next to 'im for over a week. Did he ever say anything to you 'bout who he was or where he came from?"

"No, sir, he sure didn't, not a word. And now that I think 'bout it, I bet he never said a dozen words 'bout himself the whole time. All I know for sure is he snored louder than anyone I'd ever heard before and stunk awful bad and that left eye of his never closed. My Lord the smell was terrible—and—and sometimes when he'd look at me with that messed up eye, I'd find myself wishing I was somewhere else."

"That eye does look plenty bad," Lane cut in. "I asked 'im how it came to be that way but he wouldn't tell me the truth. He tried to tell me he got drunk and rode into a low limb, but I've seen enough gunshots in my life to know he was lying."

"Yeah, I'm not a real smart man," Tater replied, "but even I've got enough sense to know a gunshot when I see it."

"Here," Lane announced, "the food's ready."

Showdown at Deer Creek 169

After the two men had eaten, Lane shook out his bedroll, and after placing his saddle at one end, he put rocks along its length, then covering them with a blanket, he placed his hat where his head should be. With that done he took up his extra blanket and started from camp.

"Where you going?" Tater asked.

"Moving a little closer to the horses," Lane answered. "And if I was you, I'd think about not beddin' down right at the fire. I'd move out a little ways and bed down somewhere in the shadows. Just because whoever it was is gone don't mean they won't come back." Turning, Lane walked in the direction of the little grassy knoll, quickly disappearing into the darkness.

At first light, Lane led the horses back to camp and while the coffee brewed, the horses were saddled and the gear picked up, and with that done, the two men sat at the fire.

"The horses got some much needed rest," Tater said.

"Not near enough," Lane replied, "but some. And I've got to admit what rest I got sure didn't do me any harm." Then he added, "we'll be back in Deer Creek tonight maybe, back to a real bed, and to some of Mrs. Mahony's fine cooking."

"That sounds awful good to me," Tater answered.

Lane stood and kicked dirt on the fire, reducing the remaining flames to just puffs of white-gray smoke. Then flipping the last few drops of coffee from the cup, he started toward the horses, and as he made his way he said, "but if we don't get started, we'll never get there."

They swung into leather, and after giving their surroundings one last look, turned and headed south. But it wasn't until they rode clear of the trees that they got a good look at all the thick, black clouds that were building along the western horizon.

"Look's like we might be in for some rain," Tater said.

"None too soon," Lane answered as he spurred his horse into a canter. "This country is mighty dry."

Bear had not rested during the night, for he could not clear his mind of the Pennington family and the manner in which they had died. And even though the trail the killers were leaving had turned south, he still had that God-awful feeling somewhere it would turn north again and lead straight to Deer Creek. Maybe not, he thought to himself, maybe it's like Mushy said and they've decided on riding the south trail into Mexico. On the other hand, who knew where men like these might be headed. It might be Waco, Austin or even San Antonio, but wherever the trail led, Bear would follow, for it was at the end of that trail, the Penningtons would finally get the justice they deserved.

"Pa," Zack called out from the fire, "if you've had your fill of coffee I reckon we're ready to put out the fire and light a shuck."

"I've had all I want," Bear called back. Stepping around his horse, he slid the Winchester down deep into the boot, then gathering the reins, he made his way to where the men waited. "We've got some dark clouds back west," he said as he walked up.

"Yes, sir. I seen 'em," Mushy answered, "and if we don't find those sorry, murdering devils or at least a little fresher trail before it rains you know as well as I do, Bear, the trail will be gone."

"You're for sure right," Bear snorted. "And there's one thing for certain we all know. We're not going to find 'em standing here talking about the clouds." Turning, he grabbed a handful of horse mane and climbed into the saddle, then looking over he said, "Zack, see if you can pick up their trail. Mavis, you, Butler, and Teal keep an eye on our back trail."

To the east the sun was just peeking over the oak covered hills and its golden rays brought a hazy glow to the somewhat muggy morning.

On the western horizon a massive wall of black-blue clouds were building and Bear knew it was just a matter of time before the rain came. He also knew that Mushy was right, that if they couldn't find the men they sought or at least a little clearer trail before it did rain what little signs there were would be gone, washed out. But the hopes of finding the killers in the near future was just that, a hope, unless they had for some reason hold-up somewhere, because with a two week or more head-start they were probably far from where Bear and the men now stood.

Zack rode a wide circle and just moments after disappearing into a small stand of willows he called out, "over here. They're still headed south."

Bear looked at his old friend and asked, "what do you think, Mushy?"

"I don't know for sure, Bear, but the signs say they're headed for Mexico."

Bear gave his head a slow, worried shake, "I sure hope you're right. I know what the signs say, but my gut tells me they're headed for Deer Creek. I don't know why, I just have a feeling that's where we're going to end up."

"You may be right, Bear," Mushy answered mildly. "But there's one thing I do know for sure. There's no way they're going to get to Deer Creek without turning back north somewhere, but for now they're moving south."

With that said the two men took to the trail in a hard lope knowing they needed to find something that would reveal the killers' final direction and maybe even their intended destination before the rain came, but as of now it looked as though Mushy was right and they were riding straight for Mexico.

By mid morning, the rising sun lay heavy upon the already dry prairie. Its bright, golden rays sucking at the land and all that grew up on it, drawing life giving moisture from whatever it touched. In doing so, many of the plants along the trail began to wilt and others that had already lost the battle, lay brown and dead on the ground. In places the earth was opened up and some of the cracks were a good foot or more wide and no telling how deep, a sure death trap for any horse that stepped in one, just another reason for a man to keep both eyes on the trail. It was already unusually hot for this time of day and with each passing moment it was getting hotter. There was no breeze to speak of, and what little air that did move was heavy and muggy. But to the west, the dark clouds grew nearer, giving promise of rain and a welcome coolness.

A far off whistle drew Bear's attention and he looked up to see Zack setting atop a distant rise, waving his hat high in the air.

"He's found something," Mushy said.

"Let's go have a look," Bear answered as he put a hard spur to his horse.

Zack threw up a pointing hand as the two men rode up. "There's a little hollow in among those oak yonder, Pa. That's where they made camp. No one around now and don't look to me like there's been anyone around for several days, but it's their camp alright, there's no doubt about that. I'd say from the way the grass is walked down and the number of empty whiskey bottles and bean cans I found scattered about that they were there for at least a week, maybe longer."

"A week," Bear echoed.

"I'd say at least that long, Pa," Zack replied with a smile, "and they could have been there longer."

"Which way were they headed when they rode out?" Mushy questioned.

"I don't know, Uncle Mushy," Zack answered. "But it shouldn't take me long to figger it out."

Bear turned in the saddle. "Mushy, you ride back and get Butler and his brothers. Me and Zack will ride on and have a look around, and we need to step about, Mushy, the rain's coming."

Hearing the order, Mushy spun his horse around and as he rode off, he threw up an understanding hand.

Bear and Zack rode in the direction of the camp and were no more than twenty-five yards out when the quiet of the mid morning was suddenly shattered by the sound of not too distant gunfire and it was coming from the same direction Mushy had just rode.

Bear quickly spun his horse, and as he spurred the animal into a dead run, he reached and drew the Winchester from its boot, then while working the action he called out in a loud voice, "Let's go Zack, we found 'em."

They rode through the oak and mesquite as fast as their horses would carry them. For nearly a half mile they rode hard but coming to a steep clay slope where the earth was scarred with wide, deep cracks they slowed to a walk and after moving past the danger they spurred their horses across a little clearing some hundred or so yards wide to a oak covered rise where they drew in to a canter, then just before reaching the top the two men reined in their horses and walked them to where they could just see over. At the bottom the Van Dill brothers had taken cover in among an outcropping of rocks and were shooting in the direction of a stand of oak no more than thirty yards west of their position but Bear's long time friend was nowhere to be seen.

"Where's Mushy?" Bear asked in a low voice.

"I don't know," Zack answered while letting his eyes quickly scan the countryside. "I don't see 'im."

Thinking the worse, Bear said. "They got 'im."

"No they didn't, Pa," Zack happily replied, then with a nod toward the west he said, "there he is. Over yonder on that ridge 'bout half way up."

Relived by the words, Bear looked to see his old friend had taken cover along a rocky ridge just west of the stand of oak and by doing so had put whoever it was in a cross fire.

"Look there, Pa." Zack said. "That ain't outlaws. It's Indians."

Bear stood tall in the saddle to have a better look, and caught only the blur of a half clothed, dark-brown body moving from one tree to another and he knew then Zack was right. It was Indians all right, probably no more than a half dozen at most and more than likely Kiowas. "We ain't got time to be messing with a bunch of Indians," Bear thought out loud to himself. Reaching down, he drew his pistol and as he did, he touched his horse forward with a hard spur. At the same instant Zack started his horse and they rode over the little rise together, riding straight for the stand of oak at a full run with their guns blazing. They had not got to within two hundred yards when the gunfire coming from the trees suddenly stopped and before they got to within a hundred yards, the Indians had mounted their horses and rode fast from the stand of oak headed north.

"Men, get your horses," Butler Van Dill called out. "We'll chase 'em into the ground."

Bear drew his horse to a sliding stop. "Just hold up there, Butler," he said. "We've got more important things to think about than a bunch of Indians."

"Where did those varmints come from?" Mushy asked riding up.

"They cut your trail 'bout five miles back," Butler answered. "We were just fixin' to move in on 'em when you came ridin' back this way and pushed 'em right in our laps."

"Glad I could be of help," Mushy said with a short chuckle. "Just tryin' to keep you boys on your toes. Wouldn't want you fellers going to sleep."

"Now that we've got the gun play out of the way," Bear cut in, "let's go have a look at that camp." Spinning his horse he lead the way back south, toward the killers camp, back to the one place he was hoping to find something that would give him a clue to where the killers were headed. To the west the dark clouds were growing thicker, and drawing nearer with each passing hour, and Bear knew, as did the rest of the men, it was just a matter of time before the rains came, rain this hot, dry, cracked land so desperately needed. It would bring life to the land and all that grew upon it. It would also add much needed water to the earth ponds and hopefully fill some of the cracks that scarred the land, but in doing so it would certainly wash out any trail the killers had left behind.

As they approached the little grove of trees, Bear reined his horse in to a walk and just at the edge of where he knew the camp to be, he drew up and slid slowly to the ground. As he tied his horse to a low hanging limb, he let his eyes quickly scan the obviously abandoned camp. The grass the killers had walked down over their many days stay here was starting to straighten, that in itself told him it had been several days since anyone had been around. He moved slowly from west to east, his eyes searching, he paused once to have a closer look at a boot track. The heel was badly run over to the outside, and it had a small *V* shaped notch dead center, apparently a mark left from stepping on a sharp rock or perhaps a piece of iron. On the far east side of the camp was a little patch of cactus where the outlaws had thrown several empty bean cans and whiskey bottles, but in among those, Bear saw something that made his face grow stiff and pale. It was nothing more than couple of jars, one was empty, but the other had what remained of a single pickled peach, and Bear knew that since his lovely wife Anna had passed, Bernice Pennington was the only one in these parts who canned pickled peaches.

Bear looked over and asked, "what do you make of it, Zack?"

Hearing the question, Zack rubbed at the week's growth of black stubble along his jaw and answered, "for sure four, Pa, maybe five men were here a week or better."

"I agree," Mushy cut in, "I'm thinking five."

"That's the way I see it," Bear replied with an agreeing nod. "Ok, men, no need in standing here jawin'. We'd better be riding." Bear turned and said, "Butler, y'all stay here with me. Zack, you and Mushy, see if you can find which way they lit out."

Both men mounted and rode from camp. Zack swung north, while Mushy rode south. Only minutes passed before Zack called out from the north side and it was then Bear knew his worse fears were coming true, the outlaws had gone north. "I just had a feeling," he said out loud to himself. "I knew somehow this deal would end up in Deer Creek."

"Ain't that where Miss Becky's supposed to be?" Butler asked worriedly.

"No, it's not," Bear answered abruptly. "She's supposed to be home by now." But as Bear stepped into leather, he had that god-awful feeling in the pit of his stomach, the feeling that his little girl was in trouble, bad trouble, maybe even dead. That awful thought for a moment took his breath, his face stiffened, and a cold chill washed over him, and his hands began to shake. "Those egg eatin' dogs better not have laid one hand on my girl," he said angrily. "If they have, there's nowhere in this whole wide world they can hide that I won't find 'em."

By the time, Bear had led the men to where Zack was walking along the trail tailing his reins, Mushy had ridden from the south. "It's as plain as the nose on my face," Zack announced, "they left here headed north."

Mushy looked over at Bear. "That don't mean they're headed for Deer Creek. There's any number of places they could be headed."

"Would you like to make a little wager on that?" Bear asked. "They're headed for Deer Creek alright, and you know it as well as I do, Mushy."

"Deer Creek can't be no more than what fifteen miles due north from here," Zack remarked.

"About that, as the crow flies," Mushy replied. "But I

wouldn't go off half cocked. I'd stay with the trail, who knows, they might change directions again."

"They ain't going to change direction, they're headed for Deer Creek, I'd stake my life on it," Bear snorted. "But you're right, Mushy, the trail's leading almost due north anyway so we might as well stay with it just in case they do change." Looking at Zack, Bear added, "take the lead, son, but we need to move quick. Your sister may be in danger."

"Ok, Pa."

Bear wiped at his brow with a rough hand, then straightened himself in the saddle and said, "let's ride," as he touched his horse with a hard spur and gave a double slap with the reins.

The sun shined hot from high in the midday sky, its brightness blinding to unshaded eyes, and its yellowish, hot glare showed little mercy on man, animal or land. In all directions, heat waves danced without direction distorting all shapes that lay beyond. To the distant east a dust devil had formed and a little further north still yet another. But to the west the great wall of black, blue clouds continued to grow, and from time to time, a far off rumble could be heard.

Bear and his men rode on, their eyes ringed red from the sun's bright glare and their shirts wet with sweat and streaked white with alkali. They all rode, up to this point with one purpose in mind, to find the killers of the Penningtons, but now they had another purpose and that was to see that Becky and the good folks of Deer Creek were safe, the latter now weighed the heaviest on Bear's mind as he rode.

The horses had already come a long way since leaving camp that morning and now they had another fifteen miles or more to go, but they were all good, strong Running T stock, and Bear knew if there was a string of horses in the country that could do it, these were the ones. But he also knew as good as they were, they all had their limits.

By mid afternoon they had covered a lot of country, rough country and the hard pace they had kept up since leaving the camp was starting to show on both men and the horses, but with Twin Mesa now in sight they knew it couldn't be no more than six miles on to Deer Creek.

"We need to pull up and let these horses rest," a voice called out, "we're killing 'em, Bear."

Bear glanced over to his old friend, and knowing he was right, drew in a bit. "We'll go on to Twin Mesa and rest 'em there, maybe even have a bite to eat and some coffee. From there it'll be a straight shot to Deer Creek." Then pointing to the western sky he added, "we're not going to make it without gettin' wet."

"Let 'er come," Mushy replied. "It looks to me like we might need to tie our hats on, too." Mushy turned his eyes to the distant mesa and his mind instantly jumped back to a cold and windy day several years ago when he and Bear had held off a little raiding party of Apaches from atop that mesa and since then it had become their regular camp site when working the cattle on this side of the ranch.

They broke over the top to find Zack squatting on his heels looking at what remained of an old burned out campfire.

Showdown at Deer Creek

"They were here," Zack said as the men rode up. "And not over a week ago, one man rode off toward the north and a few days later the rest did the same. I hate to say it, Pa, but you're right, they're headed for Deer Creek. But what I can't understand is why they didn't all ride out together?"

"You'll never be able to fully understand why men like that do what they do," Bear answered. "The only way we can even hope to break even with men of that caliber is to somehow manage to out guess 'em."

"You were right, Bear," Mushy cut in. "If we'd just cut across, we'd already be there."

"No need in second guessing ourselves, Mushy," Bear answered with a hard shake of his head. "If I'd been wrong, and you know as well as I do that I have been wrong before, where would that have put us? No, we did it right. Now we know for sure what trail they rode after they left here. So now all we've got to do is go see if they're still there." Turning to the men Bear said, "Butler, after we let the horses rest a mite I want you to ride on to the ranch and see if Becky is there. If she's not, gather all the men and meet up with us somewhere along the ridge there west of town."

"Ok, boss."

After hobbling the horses on grass, Zack gathered wood and started a fire, and Mushy started the bacon frying and while he was doing that, Butler filled the coffee pot with water from the canteen and sat it over the flames, and Teal cut the top from two cans of beans.

It was not long before they all sat around the fire eating their food, but no one was saying anything. The only sounds were those of the horses chewing as they ate the tender grass and from time to time a clap of thunder from within the nearing clouds, clouds that for the most part had now moved in and blocked out the sun's bright glare, and with the shadows came a coolness.

Bear was the first to break the silence when he said, "On second thought, Butler, you better take Mavis and Teal with you. You wouldn't stand much of a chance if you happened onto those fellers by yourself." With that said the silence came again.

Only moments had passed when all of a sudden a hard gust of wind swept across the mesa causing all at the fire to grab at their hats. "Well, it's 'bout time," Mushy called out. "We better get to our horses, men, and if you've got a slicker you better grab it, too."

"Look yonder," Bear said throwing up a hand to the west, "we'd better grab more than a slicker."

"Damn," Zack cut in. "I've never seen such a wall of rain."

"I wish you were right but what you're looking at ain't rain," Mushy said in a loud voice. "That there's hail and a lot of it." At that moment they heard the loud, roaring rumble as the chunks of ice pounding the hard ground stormed across the prairie toward them. The sky suddenly started to darken and before anyone could react, the daylight was gone and a darkness as if it was night had taken its place. The only light was that of the lightning as it streaked the darkened sky.

"Mount up men. We've got to get off this mesa," Bear called out. "We'll get under that ledge there on the east side." Then came another hard gust of wind, and not only did it blow hard but it was cold, bone chilling cold. Suddenly a few large drops of rain splattered the ground, followed by a short pause, then it was as if the whole sky opened up with a sudden windblown, blinding down pour.

With each passing moment the hail was getting closer, and Bear knew as did the rest of the men that if they didn't get to cover and fast, they were in for one terrible rough ride. They mounted and with Bear leading the way spurred their horses crossed the mesa in a dead run and just as the last man rode over the ridge the hail stones arrived with tremendous force, pounding at the earth and all that grew upon it. Lighting slapped at the far off ground with a deafening crack and another bolt struck a nearby tree causing a giant cloud of white-gray smoke and the flames of a short-lived fire.

The men had all camped at Twin Mesa at one time or other and knew the ledge was not high enough to clear a man on horseback or even a horse still saddled, nor was it big enough for all six men and horses to get under.

"I should have seen it coming," Bear yelled as he drew up. "I knew better." Stepping to the ground, he quickly unlatched the cinch then slid the saddle from the horse. With the saddle in one hand and the reins in the other he made his way under the dark, rocky ledge and as expected, there was only enough room for the men and four of the horses, but by the storm coming from the west and the men being on the east side and in close to the ledge both man and animal were all safe from the deadly hail stones which had now grown to the size of a man's fist.

"We'll be hard-pressed to find a track or anything else after this," Zack remarked.

"It makes no difference," Bear replied. "We know where they're headed. They're headed for Deer Creek."

"The only thing we don't know is," Mushy cut in, "are they still there? I don't know why they would be. Deer Creek ain't got a whole lot to offer. If George Scott has anything to do with it, they'll come up dry at the bank too."

"They ain't just thieves," Bear answered abruptly. "They're killers, and it's a proven fact they'll take a life for no reason, just look at the Penningtons back yonder. Those folks had no money or nothing else really, just a few jars of canned peaches." His mind flashed back to the three graves beside the old barn, then he mumbled, "all killed for nothing more than a dollar or two and a few jars of canned peaches."

It was a good half hour before anyone spoke again, then Zack said, "looks like the hail is lettin' up a mite, Pa."

Bear looked east through the cold, howling wind and pouring rain to see the worst of the hail had moved on but what few stones that were still falling were large and when they struck, they went deep into the rain-soaked ground. "Maybe it won't be long now," Bear suggested. "We need to be riding." At that instant a loud clap of thunder rolled across the dark, rainy sky and just above a bolt of lightening struck at the mesa, reminding them hail was not the only problem and not the only thing they had to be concerned with.

Bear rolled the situation around in his mind. The

only thing he knew about the men he sought was they were killers. Why had they gone to Deer Creek? Was it to rob the bank, as Mushy had mentioned, and if so had they done that and just rode out or had they left death behind? And where was Becky? Was she back at the ranch safe or was she maybe somewhere needing his help? He had no answers to these questions, but he knew that from Twin Mesa it was no more than six miles into town, and if the weather would just clear, he would not be long in finding out.

Chapter Eight

From within the rolling, thick, dark clouds the heavy rain continued, and one after another lightning streaked the early evening sky, and from time to time, a clap of thunder would shake the inside of the Double Deuce. Blackie nervously pushed up from his chair. There were few things in life that bothered him and the weather seemed to be one of those things for it was a situation over which he had no control and Blackie wanted control over everything. "Ain't that sheriff ever going to get back?" he asked in a loud, hard voice, as he started toward the door.

"Yeah, he'll show," R.C. answered, "I figgered he'd been here yesterday and for sure today, but I guess he's hold up somewhere because of the storm."

Blackie pushed open the batwing doors and walked out. The street stood a good half knee deep with water, and it was still raining so hard he could hardly make out the buildings across the way.

"Been one heck of a rainstorm, ain't it?"

Blackie spun at the unexpected voice to see Hank Hardin sitting in a chair leaning back on two legs against the wall. "I wish it would stop," he replied worriedly.

"It'll be a while yet," Hank answered knowingly. "Those clouds are thick and tall, but it looks to me like the worst of the weather went south of us. It hailed over that way, maybe even one of those twisters."

"How do you figger that?" Blackie asked. "Don't tell me you've got one of those crystal balls you can look into."

"No, Blackie, I don't have a crystal ball," Hank said with a laugh. "I can sometimes tell just by looking at the clouds, the way they're turning and all, and those big white ones you can almost bet had hail in 'em, and the cold wind is another sign. Although I don't really know for sure, I'd say there's ice falling somewhere close by."

"What makes the hail?" Blackie asked, "You got any idea?"

"Don't rightly know," Hank answered. "But one time up at Wichita I saw some stones as big as a supper plate. Came crashing right through the roof it did, tore up the town and killed a whole passel of the people and livestock, and hurt a sight more."

"Through the roof?" Blackie questioned. "I can't hardly believe that, Hank. What had you been drinking, some of that Traveling Sideshow Elixir?"

"No, sir, I hadn't been drinking at all." Hank answered,

then gesturing toward his face with two fingers he said, "right through the roof, it surely did, Blackie. I seen it with my own two eyes. I was there and seen it."

"I'll have to say that's one heck of a story," Blackie admitted with a chuckle, "but I don't know whether I should believe it or not. Ice coming through the roof of a building, now that's some pretty powerful stuff. But whether you're telling it true or feeding me a yarn, it's well worth a drink. Come on in and I'll buy you one."

Hank waved off the invitation and replied, "I better stay out here and keep watch. That sheriff should be getting back anytime."

Blackie jerked his head toward the door and said, "come on in and have a drink, Hank. We don't have to worry 'bout anybody showing up now, not in this storm. A person would have to be running from a posse swinging a hang noose to travel in this weather."

Hank suddenly jumped to his feet and in the same motion, threw the tail of his slicker back and stood looking along the boardwalk far beyond where Blackie stood.

"Hold your fire," a voice said. "It's me."

"Putman," Blackie called out with a laugh, "We'd given you up for drowned."

"Almost did, Blackie, I've been up in the loft of the livery," Truitt answered. "That thing's leaking like it ain't even got a roof on it. I got wet and cold so I thought I'd come warm up a mite, maybe even have a drink or two."

Again a bright, jagged bolt of lightning lit up the sky with a deafening crack and the thunder that followed

Showdown at Deer Creek

seem to shake the boardwalk. Blackie ducked from the loud, nerve shaking sound and hurriedly pushed back inside.

Becky and Mrs. Mahony were changing the bandage on Sam Stovall's wound and glanced up when the men entered.

"Come on over, sit, and have a drink," Blackie said as he dropped down into the chair.

R.C. gave each man a welcoming nod as they walked up, and as Truitt took a seat, R.C. slid the bottle in his direction. "Here," he said. "Looks like you might be needin' a little something to knock the chill." Looking over at Blackie he added, "I've 'bout got a gut full of this place."

"I'd had more than my fill the first day," Blackie replied. "We'll be riding out tomorrow whether the sheriff shows or not. We can always come back and take care of him. What we really need to do is sell the girl to her pappy. I'm a-thinking 'bout loadin' her up and ridin' out that way in the morning, and while we're out there we can see 'bout taking care of that old loud-mouth cowboy, that Mushy Crabtree."

R.C. gave an agreeing nod and said, "now you're talking, Blackie. If you ask me, that's what we should have done days ago."

Blackie's face instantly flashed dark with anger. Then propping his elbow onto the table, he leaned across and said through gritted teeth, "nobody asked you, R.C., and it would be best for you to remember who's runnin' this outfit. The rules are the same simple one's we've always had. We'll stay when I say stay, and we'll go when and where I say go, not until, and we'll kill when I say somebody needs killin'."

"I know you're the boss, hell we all do, Blackie," R. C. said as he slowly stood up from the table. "I was just saying we need to be clear of this town." At the door he stopped and looked back, "I'm going to have a look around."

Truitt watched him go, then turning slowly toward Blackie he asked, "were you serious 'bout killin' all these people and burnin' the town?"

"Yes, I was. We're going to kill every last one of 'em, and burn the town down just like I said. I want people to know, and remember what happens when they lock Blackie Getts up. No, sir, nobody treats Blackie Getts any such way and lives to tell about it. Nobody, and you can believe me when I say I'm going to kill that do-gooder sheriff, too."

Truitt had heard Charlie Hennessey say on any number of occasions that Blackie Getts was one dangerous *hombre*. As bad as they come. He had years ago crossed the line from being a man who would think things out to just a cold blooded killer, a man who took what he wanted at any cost. Charlie had also said one time that taking a person's life weighed less on Blackie than any man he'd ever seen or heard of, and even though he liked Blackie, it was better to stay clear of him because he was out of his mind mean. But Truitt had not realized just exactly what his old boss had meant until now. Now it was obvious that at first light they would kill every breathing soul in this town and

Showdown at Deer Creek 191

then burn it down. Truitt was not sure he wanted to take part in any such a massacre, but he had hired on to take orders, and he knew if he tried to ride out now, Blackie or one of the others would surely kill him.

Along a narrow trail some miles north of town, lightning for an instant lit up the dark, stormy sky to reveal two men on horseback. Both were tired and hungry and soaked to the skin from the relentless rain. Their muscles ached from the long, hard ride, and their bodies shivered from the wet cold. Still they rode on through the blinding rain, earth shaking thunder, and never ending lightning over a trail that ran well above ankle deep in water. In among the trees in which they made their way the western horizon was mostly blocked from view, but from time to time there were openings and looking west revealed no breaks in the dark clouds anywhere.

Lane Tipton pulled his collar tight trying to stop the cold rain from running down his back, but the attempt didn't seem to help and even though he had a good slicker, there was just too much rain falling for it to shed.

Suddenly, lightning struck within the top branches of a not too distant tree with a loud, ear piercing crack and the force sent limbs crashing to the ground. Flames and white smoke quickly rose but the heavy rain drove them back down, at the same instant a loud roar of thunder rolled across the dark sky.

"We're pushing our luck," Tater hollered, "we gotta get out away from all these trees."

"There's a clearing just up ahead," Lane called back. But as he spoke the words, he knew from where they now rode it could not be over three maybe four miles to Deer Creek and unless the storm got a lot worse, or his horse somehow came up lame, he had no intentions of stopping at the clearing or anywhere else. After three long days of wondering and speculation it was time to find out if the man he had left in his jail was the same Blackie Getts that Sheriff Moore had told him about. And if indeed he was the same man, was he still in jail with Tom Walker looking after him or had his gang rode in and busted him out like they had done down at Presidio. And if something like that had occurred in what condition had they left Tom Walker, the town, and the people in it? "No," Lane mumbled out loud, and then he thought, as much as I'd like to, and as bad as the horses need a rest, I don't reckon I'll be stopping until I get there.

By the time they had rode clear of the brush, the storm had let up a little, and even though the rain continued to pour, the thunder and lightning had lessened. But looking west, it was evident by the great mass of black-blue clouds the storm was nowhere close to being over.

Tater stepped to the ground, but noticing Lane still in the saddle he looked up and asked, "what's wrong? Ain't you going to get down?"

Rain poured from the brim of Lane's hat. "No, I think I'll ride on," he said with a quick jester toward the south, "but Tater, you stay if you want to. I know with the lightning striking everywhere it'll be safer out here in the open than in among the trees."

Showdown at Deer Creek

"No, sir," Tater replied shaking his head. "If you ain't stayin' then I ain't stayin'." Turning, he crawled back into the wet saddle and once he had adjusted himself, he looked over and said, "lead out."

Lane knew they should stay in the clearing, and riding back into the trees during a lightning storm was against his better judgment, and against all that Bear Townsend, and Mushy Crabtree had taught him, but the awful feeling that kept gnawing at his insides told him he needed to be in Deer Creek and it was because of that one single feeling he spun his horse and started south.

It was getting along to late evening when they drew up atop a rise just a little over a mile north of town and at the bottom was the trail leading from Deer Creek northeast to Fort Worth. The very same trail they had ridden ten days before, but now it was more like a raging river than a trail. Lane knew just east of town most of the water would turn into the little gully and flow south eventually dumping into Deer Creek but what water the gully could not handle, would spill over and move on west straight through town making the street impassable. "We're almost there," he said to Tater.

"We just can't go riding in," Tater replied, "without making sure what we're up against, if anything."

"No, you're right," Lane answered. "I'm not hankering to go ridin' into any trap. Just to be on the safe side we'll swing west and ride along the ridge. There's a rocky bluff over on the northwest side where we can see the town." After taking a little time to think he added, "But with it raining this hard a person might not be able to see much from there." The two men turned and rode off in that direction, but Lane suddenly drew in his horse and when Tater rode alongside he said, "If you can't get a good look from the bluff we'll go on west another half mile. There's a place where Becky and I sometimes go to picnic. It's up on a hill just north of the schoolhouse; from there you can see the whole town, from one end to the other right down the middle of the street."

A short time later they made their way to the edge of the bluff and as expected all that could be seen was a much rain-blurred gray outline of the town, but Lane could make out enough to know with darkness so quickly approaching there were not enough lanterns lit along the street, but he also knew, with the high wind and heavy rain they might have been lit earlier and since then gotten blown out. But if that was the case it was surely not like Evret McNare, whose job it was to see the lanterns all got lit in the first place, to leave them out. Lane noticed one more thing that made his suspicion rise even more. No light of any kind could be seen around the livery stable inside or out and it was usually one of the most well lit places in town. Still with it not completely dark yet and with the heavy rain obstructing his view, light could very well be there and he was just not seeing it. Looking over at Tater, he said, "let's go on around and have a look from the other side."

The two men worked their way on west, through the dense oak, mesquite, and small patches of scrub cedar, then coming to an outcropping of boulders, some standing as much as three feet taller than a man's head on horseback, Lane turned and rode south, but now with each passing moment it was growing darker and not because the clouds were blocking out the sun, but because night was upon them. After about a hundred yards or so they rode in among a small stand of towering cottonwood, and from there they turned and rode back east to where the trail opened into a small clearing some fifty yards wide and maybe half that distance across. When the lightning came again, Tater noticed a giant old oak standing out by itself on the farside, and for some strange reason he kind of figured it was to that old tree they were headed. But it wasn't until Lane drew up under its low hanging limbs and slid from the saddle that Tater knew for sure.

"You sure can," Tater said as he walked up.

"You sure can what?" Lane asked.

"See the whole town," Tater replied, "but it would help if this rain would let up a mite."

Lane looked as best he could through the pouring rain for any sign of life along the street of Deer Creek. Then after a long careful study he turned and said, "I don't know 'bout this deal, Tater. The town's awful quiet."

"Maybe everyone is just inside out of the weather."

"This is a bad storm alright," Lane answered quietly. "But still, it just don't look right to me. I've never seen it to where someone wasn't moving about somewhere, and there's no lanterns lit at the livery at all. No, there's something wrong, I'd stake my life on it."

"Maybe we should move on down hill aways to have a better look," Tater suggested.

Lane studied what Tater had said, and after giving it some thought, he answered, "no. I want you to stay here. I'll go down and have a look around, but if I'm not back in a couple of hours I want you to ride out to the Running T and tell Bear Townsend to bring his men." Lane paused to think then added, "just south of here about two maybe three hundred yards you'll cut a trail. If you follow it west it'll lead straight to the ranch. It's a big two-story house, and the only house between here and there, you can't miss it."

"I don't know, Sheriff," Tater said. "If Blackie and his gang are down there, you'll be needin' help."

"I'm just going to have a look, that's all, just to see what we're up against. But if something does happen, there's no need in us both gettin' caught up in it." With that said, Lane crawled back into the saddle, then looking down he added, "if you go, don't try to cross Deer Creek at Tubs Crossing. The water will be too wide and fast. Ride on north about a mile, there's a place where the creek runs under a narrow ridge of cap-rock. It'll be easy to find because with this much rain, it'll be making a loud sucking sound as the water goes through. It's just wide enough for a sure-footed horse to cross so you'll have to be careful." Then nudging his horse forward, Lane started down the hill quickly disappearing into the rainy darkness.

"I should have gone with him," Tater mumbled to himself, "but he said stay here." When the lightning

Showdown at Deer Creek 197

came again, Tater looked in the direction Lane had gone but unable to see anything but trees, he turned and started from under the oak knowing it would be safer out in the open. Luckily he did not have to go far before he came upon what remained of giant old cottonwood deadfall and knew if he could get in close to the trunk it would not protect him from the rain so much but it would block some of the cold wind. Tying his horse to one of the exposed roots he started working his way among the limbs until he found a place he could sit and still have a clear view of the tree where he knew Lane would come back to. He pulled his collar tight and after adjusting his hat to shield him from the rain he settled in for the long wait.

Lane rode slowly toward the town staying well within the trees. He knew if Blackie Getts and his men had for some reason taken over Deer Creek there would be guards posted, and for sure if they had any sense, there'd be at least one in the loft of the livery stable watching the east trail. Lane knew too, there would surely be gunplay if the outlaws spotted him. If that did happen, and he found himself needing to get away fast, he would need his horse close to hand. That meant leaving him tied in a location where he would not only be close by, but also out of sight and that could only be one place, behind Sam Stovall's saddle shop where the brush-line was no more than twenty yards from the back door. But it would be while crossing those twenty yards and he'd have no cover of any kind until he reached the back of the building, and if someone happened to be looking at the right instant and a flash of lightning lit up the night they might see him. "I'll have to stay low and move fast," he mumbled to himself.

As Lane drew closer the rain, lightning and thunder continued to dominate the dark sky. The wind blew hard from the west and it howled and moaned as it pushed its way past, forcing all it came in contact with to bend and sway and shake and in doing so causing a never ending sea of unfamiliar sounds and movements. Realizing the storm had taken away two very important senses, the ability to spot slight movement, and to distinguish between sounds that did or did not belong, he eased on knowing if danger did lie ahead, Blackie and his gang would have to deal with the same losses in hearing and seeing he was dealing with.

At the edge of the brush, Lane drew up and sat while letting his eyes search the darkness all along the back of the buildings, then along the roofs, and then each window and door for anything that might tell him someone was watching. It was a long, careful study and when satisfied, he slowly slid from the saddle. Not wanting to take the chance on the reins maybe giving way in case of a nearby lightning strike and the hose running off, he took the rope from his saddle and placing it around the horse's neck, tied him off securely to a tree trunk. He checked the Winchester first, then reaching down he drew his pistol, flipped open the cylinder and gave it a spin making sure it had a full load, then pushing it back into the holster, he slipped the leather thong over the hammer.

Turning his attention back to the dark, rainy sky, Lane

tried to time the lightning. He knew with such a short amount of time between them he would have to be ready to make his move when the lightning came and move fast across the clearing if he stood any chance of reaching cover before the lightning came again. He let his eyes quickly survey the situation and after finding nothing had changed, he pulled his hat down tight and focused on the narrow entrance of the alley between the saddle shop and hardware store and at the moment the lightning lit up the dark sky, Lane took a deep breath and started from the brush in a dead run. He had no more than got started when he stubbed his toe on something and splashed hard to the ground, but quickly getting back to his feet, he moved on across the clearing but at less than half way he stepped into an unseen water-filled hole that caused him to stumble, but after somehow regaining his balance he continued on, and the next time he slowed he was well within the dark shadows of the alleyway.

For a long moment he stood holding his breath, trying to hear, but the only sounds were that of the thunder and falling rain, and from somewhere down the street a shutter squeaked back and forth in the wind and from time to time it would bang shut. Hunkered down and moving one foot at a time, he moved slowly along the wall of the hardware store in the direction of the dimly lit street, on occasions having to feel his way in the darkness around farm implements and wagon wheels Lamar Tuggle kept stacked along the wall. It was only when the lightning came and lit up the dark alley did he have any sight whatsoever and only then for just that one split second, but Lane knew the alley well and the small amount of light the lightning produced was enough to get him to where he was going, and that was to the rain barrel sitting beside the boardwalk where the alley opened up onto the street. It was from there he knew he could see much of the town, and too, in behind the barrel he would be out of sight. Just a few feet from his destination the sound of a distant voice caused all movement to stop. He quickly looked to his left along the street and his pulse quickened when he saw that someone, a stranger had emerged from the batwing doors of the Double Deuce, then as the man started along the boardwalk in his direction, Lane moved his finger over the trigger of the Winchester.

"Hey," the man called out. "How did you get across this river?"

Thinking the man had surely seen him and was asking him the question, Lane started to speak, but before he could, he heard another voice answer, "in front of the hotel down there, someone has laid out some boards." Hearing the unexpected voice made the hair on Lane's neck stand out straight, and a cold chill suddenly washed over him because the voice that had answered was just a few feet away, probably someone sitting on the bench in front of the hardware store.

The man who came from the saloon walked on and when he was out of sight, Lane moved in behind the rain barrel and dropped down to one knee. He listened closely, trying to hear the man in front of the hardware store move, or breathe, or do anything that would tell him his exact location, but the rain and thunder along with the rain running from the roof and splashing into the overrunning rain barrel made it impossible. Lane

Showdown at Deer Creek 201

did hear footsteps coming along the boardwalk as the other man approached.

"Seen anything?" The man asked.

"Nope," the second man answered, "nothing but water."

"I'm headed back to the livery," the first man said. "I'll go anywhere to get away from Blackie. I hate to say it, but Charlie was right. Blackie don't care 'bout nothin' but killin' and making people pay and gettin' even."

There was a long moment of silence then the second man said, "I remember when Blackie was a good leader. Back in those days, we pulled a lot of small jobs and made a lot of money, but now, but now it's just like this deal here. Look at all the days we've wasted here waiting on that sheriff to get back just because Blackie wants to kill 'im. And I see no good reason to burn the town, but we will because Blackie wants it done, and for sure there's absolutely no reason to kill all these people, but I'll guarantee you, Putman, at first light that's exactly what's going to happen."

"R. C., you know," Putman started, "the law ain't going to let us get by with anything like that. Every lawman in this part of the country will be after us. No, sir, there'll be no place for us to hide. Not even in Mexico."

"I know," R. C. replied quietly, and after a short pause he added, "but anyway, Putman, you'd better get along to the livery. If Blackie hears you talking any such way you won't have to wait for the law to kill you. He'll do it for 'em."

"It don't matter," Putman replied. "If I don't get some dry clothes I'm goin' to catch my death, and if the weather don't kill me the smell of all those dead bodies piled up in that stall will."

Lane heard footsteps start in his direction and just before the man came into view, he hunkered more closely to the barrel. Stepping from the boardwalk, the outlaw sloshed his way across the muddy alley to the other side then on down boardwalk toward the livery. Lane listened as the footsteps faded into the rainy night and when they had, he thought back on what had been said. It was clear that Blackie Getts had been busted out of jail and for the past several days he and his gang had been riding roughshod over the town while waiting on Lane to get back so Blackie could kill him. Furthermore, they were planning to kill all the towns folk and set the town ablaze at first light. And from what the one called Putman had said there were already dead bodies piled up in a stall at the livery stable. Who or how many, Lane had no idea, but it was clear that at daylight there would be a lot more. Lane had also heard enough to know there were at least three outlaws, the two that were just talking and Blackie Getts, but how many more, he did not know. But that was something Lane needed to find out, and not only how many, but also their location and too, the location of the towns folk. Again he let his eyes move quickly along the street but unable to see anything that might give him a clue, he decided to move to where he could see into the Double Deuce and that meant entering the Longhorn Cafe which matched up door to door with the saloon directly across the street.

Lane made his way slowly back along the alley, then along the backs of the building to the back door of the

Showdown at Deer Creek

cafe. For a long moment he stood listening as best he could for sound, a voice or footstep or anything that might alert him to someone being inside, but unable to hear anything he slowly removed his hat and raised his head until he could peer through a narrow gap between the old burlap curtains hanging over one of the badly weather-stained windows. Rain ran down the windowpane and he wiped at it, trying to get a clear view of the inside, but all he could see was a rain-blurred darkness.

Slowly he reached down and quietly turned the handle only to find the door, as expected, was locked. Knowing there was but one thing he could do, he waited for the next roll of thunder and when it came, he slammed his shoulder hard against the door and the latch instantly gave way. With his Winchester at the ready, he slowly made his way across to the stove to find it only warm to the touch, leading him to believe it had not been used since sometime earlier today, maybe as long ago as breakfast. At the double doors leading into the front, he paused again to listen, but after hearing nothing but rain falling on the roof, he eased one side open and entered. Only a dim glimmer of light shined through the windows nearest the street, but there was luckily enough light that when the lightning came, he could make his way around the tables and chairs without bumping into any. As he approached the windows, he removed his hat and dropped down to his hands and knees on the floor and crawled slowly into position to see out. He let his eyes move quickly along the boardwalk taking in all they could.

The first thing he noticed out of place was light coming from many of the windows along the upstairs of the

Madison House Hotel and Lane found that strange for he had never known of the hotel ever having over three or four guests at any one time, but from where he sat, it was as though all the rooms were occupied and Lane even thought he had seen shadows move across one or two of the windows. Suddenly, movement caught his attention, and he let his eyes move quickly back to the brightly lit window directly across the way and even through the pouring rain, he did not have to look twice to know who he was looking at: it was the badly disfigured face of Blackie Getts. He was sitting at the little table nearest the window having a drink and across from him sat another man that Lane had never seen before. At the sight of the two men, Lane tightened his grip on the Winchester, but quickly realizing the way the outlaws were scattered he would be lucky to get one or maybe both of them before the others discovered his location and moved in. "No," he mumbled to himself, "me getting myself killed will do no one any good. I need help, I need Bear Townsend and the men from the Running T." Knowing what he had to do, Lane started to move slowly back from the window when something else caught his eye. It was a movement just beyond where Blackie was sitting. Lane wiped the water from his eyes with a wet sleeve and looked again and when he finally realized what he was looking at, an awful sick feeling instantly washed over him and he froze dead in his tracks. "Becky, Mrs. Mahony," he mumbled under his breath. And they seemed to be doing something but Lane had no idea what until Mrs. Mahony moved to her right. "Sam, that's Sam Stovall and from the looks of things he's been wounded," he said to himself.

Knowing there couldn't be no more than eight hours before daylight, Lane knew he would have to ride fast and hard if he was going make it to the Running T, get Bear Townsend and his men, and get back before the killings took place. But he also knew the horses had already been pushed well past their limits and like him, they were worn out. Then he thought, what if Bear ain't there or what if my horse steps in a hole and breaks a leg. *No, I can't take the chance of not getting back. I need to stay here. Maybe me and Tater can somehow get the job done. It won't be easy, but I know where the outlaws are located, and I know there's at least four, at least four, but I don't know for sure if that's all of them or not.* Still on his hands and knees, Lane moved slowly back into the shadows and when he was certain he could stand without being seen, he did and started for the back door. Outside he backtracked to where he'd left the horse but just as he started to step into leather, a voice spoke from the darkness.

"Old pardner, you make one wrong move and I'll blow a hole in you. I can put my fist through."

Lane did as directed, but thinking he recognized the voice he said, "Uncle Mushy, I sure hope that's you."

"Lane," the voice said, "I was thinking that looked like you coming across there but in the dark and with this rain falling I didn't know for sure."

Lane turned and as he did lightning flashed and lit up the face of his Uncle Mushy. "Where's Bear?" Lane asked.

"He'll be along shortly. Him and Zack are back yonder aways keeping company with a sidewinder they caught hiding in among the limbs of a dead tree. He says he's riding with you. Says his name is Tater of all things."

Lane gave a half-hearted chuckle. "Yeah, that's his name alright." Then he added. "Uncle Mushy, we've got a problem. The town's been taken over by a bunch of outlaws."

"I know," Mushy answered. "They killed the Penningtons over at Indian Springs. We've been tracking 'em for better than a week. That's how we ended up here in the middle of this rainstorm."

"That ain't the worst of it," Lane replied. "They've got Becky. I saw her, Mrs. Mahony and Sam through the window of the Double Deuce."

"I kinda figured as much," Mushy answered. "Bear was hoping she'd left for home, but I think in the back of his mind he knew."

"I counted four," Lane said.

"There's five of 'em. Or at least we've been following five sets of tracks."

"One of 'em is Blackie Getts," Lane said. "The man you saw shoot the drifter that night in the Double Deuce."

"That explains why one set of tracks left camp before the others did."

The lightning came again to reveal three men coming on horseback.

"I've never been so happy to see anyone in my life," Lane said to Bear as the men rode up. "They've got

Becky, Bear and I heard 'em say there's bodies in the livery and they're going to kill 'em all at sunup, then burn the town down."

"Well, we're here to see if we can change their plans," Bear replied as he stepped to the ground, then turning, he took Lane's hand. "It's good to see you, son. Have you seen her? Is Becky alright?"

"Yes, I have, but no more than ten minutes ago," Lane answered. "They've got her there in the saloon along with Mrs. Mahony and Sam Stovall. He's wounded, how bad I don't know." Lane paused to think then added, "there's two of 'em in the saloon, one sitting on the bench in front of Lamar Tuggle's hardware store, and another up in the loft of the livery. If there's a fifth, I don't know where he's at. All I know is I saw three and heard one more talking."

"There's five alright," Bear said. "That is if one ain't gone and got himself killed somehow."

"If he's alive, he may be somewhere around the hotel. That's where it looks to me like they're holding the rest of the towns folk," Lane said.

"And you say there's two of 'em in the saloon with Becky?" Bear asked.

"Yes, sir. Blackie Getts, the leader and one more. Both sitting at the table just left of the batwing doors and nearest the window. They're just sitting there drinking, like they ain't got anything to worry about."

"Oh, they've got plenty to worry 'bout," Mushy broke in. "They just don't know it yet."

"What we've got to do is take care of the two in the

saloon first," Bear said worriedly. "We don't want 'em hurtin' Becky, or nobody else for that matter."

Mushy looked at his old friend and asked, "what you got in mind?"

"Well," Lane cut in, "we need to draw those two inside the saloon outside and at the same time get someone in there to block their way if they try to get back in."

"Lane," Bear said, "why don't you work around, and when I draw 'em out, you see about getting in." He paused to think then added, "Mushy, you take care of the one in front of the hardware store and that will also put you in position to see anybody coming from the hotel." Then he gave Zack a smile and nod, and said, "Son, you go get the one in the loft at the livery."

"Ok, Pa."

"What about me?" Tater asked. "I didn't ride all that way in this weather just to stand here and hold the horses."

Lane looked over and said, "Tater, you come with me." Then turning to Bear he asked, "how are we going to go 'bout gettin' 'em to come out?"

"The only way I know," Bear answered. "I'm going to give you time to get in place, then I'm going to ride up to the hitch rail like I own the place."

"I don't know," Mushy said. "You do that and they'll kill you for sure, Bear."

"You may be right, Mushy, they sure might, but that's Becky they've got in there, and we've got to get 'em outside. Now if you've got a better idea, let's hear it."

Showdown at Deer Creek

There was a long silence then Mushy said, "I'll ride in. At least I'll make a smaller target."

Bear Townsend put out his wet hand and his old friend took it, "No, sir," he said. "I do thank you for the fine offer, Mushy, but you just take care of the one at the hardware store." Then turning back he said, "now y'all go on and get in position. I'll give you time to get settled, then I'll ride in from the schoolhouse."

"Bear," Lane said, "I think you're making a mistake riding in there like that. If anybody should ride in it should be me."

"I've made 'em before, mistakes that is," Bear answered with a shallow smile, "and they've always managed to somehow work out in my favor." Then in a low voice he added, "Lane, when this deal is done, if for some reason I don't make it back to the ranch, I want to know that you'll take care of my Becky."

"You know I will, Bear. Becky means more to me than anything else in this world."

"Ok, son. Now you go on and let's see if we can get this town back, or at least what's left of it."

Lane knew that because one of the outlaws was in the loft at the livery stable, he and Tater would have to cross the street west of there to be out of his sight, but then there was the one in front of the hardware store and though it was pitch black where Lane had decided to cross, he knew an ill-timed streak of lightning would light up the whole street as if it was daylight and anyone looking at that instant would surely see them.

At the entrance of the alley Mushy broke from the

group and disappeared into the dark shadows. Zack led the men east along the back of the buildings then noticing something strange as he approached the west corral of the livery stable, he drew up and turning to Lane he said in a low voice. "I wonder whose idea it was to put those mules over on this side."

"I don't know," Lane answered. "But it sure wasn't Evret McNare. We know that much." With that said, Zack walked on east while Lane and Tater turned south and made their way along the corral fence toward the street.

Lane had never seen so much rain in all his life, although he had on a few occasions over the years seen water up to the first step along the boardwalk, he had never seen it up to the third step as it was now and with the rain still falling, the water was sure to rise even more. It was through that unnatural river of muddy water that Lane planned to cross the street. Turning to Tater he said, "we need to stay low, maybe plum down on our bellies when we cross, but be sure to keep your pistol up clear of the water."

"Ok," Tater replied.

Lane dropped to his hands and knees and started to crawl and as the water deepened, its force against his body grew. At one point he lost his footing and the rushing water swept him down stream a good ten yards or more, but he was somehow able to get his feet dug back into the mud and come to a stop. Time and again lightning lit up the town and thunder rolled without end across the dark sky. Quickly he wiped the water from his eyes as best he could and looked through the falling rain

Showdown at Deer Creek

in the direction of the bench in front of the hardware store to see if the outlaw there had spotted him, but saw nothing but darkness. He had to push hard against the fast moving water to keep his footing, but several times he slipped and each time he was washed further and further toward the middle of town, making it easier for the killers to spot him. Finally coming to a water trough, he reached out and grabbed hold, bringing himself to a stop. Moments later, he emerged on hands and knees from the rushing waters at the northeast corner of the barbershop, not stopping until he was well out of sight. There he sat flat and while he waited on Tater to come along, he dumped the water out of his boots.

"I sure thought you were a goner," Tater said quietly.

"If it hadn't been for that water trough being where it was I would have been," Lane answered, then said, "you'd better dump the water out of your boots. I could hear them sloshing way before I could see you." Lane glanced up at the open door of the loft and as expected, was unable to see anything, but the lack of hollering and shooting told him the guard posted there had not seen them and satisfied with the outcome, Lane turned and started along the back of the buildings in the direction of the Double Deuce. Just before reaching their destination, Lane drew up, then looking at Tater he whispered, "when we hear the shot we want to hit that door hard, Tater. I mean with everything we've got. We'll only have one chance and it may have a bolt over it so we've got to hit it hard."

Lane paused then added. "If we don't get in there on the first try a lot of innocent people are going to die."

"We'll get through it," Tater replied.

At the steps leading up to the back door Lane paused, and turning to Tater he whispered, "I'll move on around to the side to where I'll be in position to see Bear coming along the street and when I do I'll come back."

"Ok," Tater answered with a nod.

Slowly, Lane made his way toward the street and each time he passed under a window, he found himself wanting to look in, but afraid someone might spot him and spoil the plan, he moved on until he got to where he could see along the street going west. Suddenly from behind, gunshots rang out and he spun, but knowing he didn't have time to get back to where Tater was, Lane slapped at the windowpane with the barrel of his rifle and just as the man who had been sitting with Blackie started to stand, Lane let a shot go, striking the man in the chest then working the lever as fast as he could, he pulled the trigger again. The bullets ripped at the man's upper body forcing him hard against the wall. He tried desperately to draw his gun, but had no more than cleared leather when he pulled off a shot that went deep into the floor, then he slowly started to slide down the wall, and when he came to rest on the floor, he was dead.

"Lane!" Becky called out.

Lane quickly let his eyes scan the room but Blackie Getts was nowhere to be seen. "Where's Blackie?" he asked through the window.

"I don't know," Becky answered. "He went out the back door a good bit ago."

Showdown at Deer Creek 213

From the direction of the livery stable four shots rang out, and from across the street, still another and a few seconds later, two more from across the street.

Realizing the shooting had started in the back, Lane ran in that direction to find Tater lying on the porch with a gunshot wound to his right arm. "What happened?" he asked.

"I don't know," Tater answered. "I was waiting for you to come back when Getts came out of the outhouse. I think he's hit but I'm not sure," Tater said, then giving his head a nod toward the west he added, "he took off that way."

"How bad are you hit?" Lane asked.

"Not bad," Tater answered. "I think the bullet went all the way through."

Knowing he needed to check on Becky and the others, Lane stepped around Tater and through the door to find Becky had already stripped the gun and holster from the dead body of the outlaw and was latching it in place.

"Where's Blackie?" she asked.

"Headed west," Lane answered. Then taking Becky in his arms, he gave her a light little kiss on her badly bruised lips. Then he pulled her close and just held her. That's how they were when Mushy and Zack came through the batwing doors. "I got the one in front of the hardware store and took two shots at another in front of the hotel, but a support pole got in the way. You were right Lane, the hotel is where they're holding the rest of the towns folk."

"I got the one up in the loft," Zack said as he embraced his sister. "And as I was headin' out, I noticed two wagons loaded with everything from clothes to guns, and I found a stall with several dead bodies in it."

"They've killed six," Becky said, "including one of their own."

"Becky," Lane started, "There's a man shot in the arm out back. If you and Mrs. Mahony will look after him, we'll go see about rounding-up the rest of 'em."

"No," Becky replied, "I want to go with you. Where's Pa?"

At that instant, the report of two more shots came from the west.

Lane broke for the back door in a dead run. "Come on men. Bear's got 'em at the schoolhouse." But before he went out he turned and said, "if you would Becky, I really need you to stay here and help Mrs. Mahony look after the injured man. There's enough of us to take care of what's left of the outlaws."

Lane led the men west through the mud and rain toward the schoolhouse where he was sure the shots had come from. The location became even more apparent when a streak of lightning lit up the night to reveal Bear sitting horseback in among some trees just east of the little brown building. "What happened?" Bear asked as the men approached. "I thought you were going to wait until I rode in? How's Becky? Is she alright?"

"I'll tell you about it later," Lane answered. "And yes, Becky's just fine. She's scared, but she's ok."

"He ran into the school," Bear said, "I shot twice, but didn't get a clear shot either time."

"Was it Getts?" Lane asked.

"I don't know," Bear answered. "I've never seen Getts. All I know is I saw the outline of a man running and took a shot."

"There's another one here some place," Mushy cut in.

"Becky!" Lane shouted. Spinning in his tracks, he started back toward the Double Deuce in a dead run.

Becky and Mrs. Mahony had gotten Tater to his feet and moved him inside where they laid him on the bar. The bullet had only nicked his arm, but high up on the bicep so there was little to do other than try to stop the bleeding, then wrap it with strips of cloth torn from an apron Mrs. Mahony had found behind the bar. That job was almost finished when Becky noticed Mrs. Mahony's face suddenly go pale, and she lost all expression.

"I should have sold you to Stillwell the first day," a voice said from behind. A voice that to Becky was all too familiar; it was the voice of Blackie Getts.

"You should have," Becky replied then added, "I can't believe I didn't smell you come in."

"Why you little . . ."

"What you going to do, Blackie, shoot me in the back?" Becky asked.

"I should!" Blackie screamed. "And I should shoot that cook, too."

"That would really make you a big man," Becky said with a laugh. "Shooting two women in the back would show everybody what kind a man you really are." Then Becky spun to face him and said, "I can beat you, Blackie. I know it and so do you. I'm faster than you are and I'm a woman."

"You're crazy. Ain't no girl faster on the draw than me."

"I am. And I'll prove it if you'll holster your gun." There was a long silence then Becky said, "what's wrong, Blackie you afraid of being killed by a woman?"

"I ain't afraid of nobody, man or woman, and especially no woman."

"I think you are, Blackie. I think you know if you holster that gun I'll kill you." Then Becky took a couple of steps to her left, getting clear of Tater and Mrs. Mahony. "Well, what's it going to be Blackie? You going to shoot me down in cold blood like you have all the others, or are you going to prove to me how fast you are?"

Blackie's face grew dark with anger and he said, "I came back to get you so I could sell you as a whore down in Mexico, but now you've stepped over the line, girl. On my worse day I can still out draw you." Slowly he thumbed the hammer down on the Colt and shoved it into the holster. "But now I think you'd be better off dead. So go on. It's your play, Little Missy," he said through gritted teeth.

"Oh, no, I want you to draw first, Blackie. I don't want you telling anybody I tricked you or you gave me the edge."

Blackie let out a loud, roaring belly laugh and said, "if you're going to be doing all the killing then who am I going to be telling?" At the same instant he dropped his hand for his pistol.

But he was nowhere near fast enough and before he could even clear leather, one shot ripped at his heart and the second struck him dead center of his belly.

Showdown at Deer Creek

Blackie's face instantly filled with surprise then it went blank and he staggered back on stiff legs. He tried hard to speak but only blood flowed from his mouth. For in that instant, Blackie Getts knew he was still standing, but at the same instant he knew he was a dead man and that a woman had killed him.

"When you get to hell," Becky shouted, "You can tell the devil himself."

Blackie stood for a bit longer as if he was defying death, but with life quickly slipping away, his knees buckled and he fell face down on to the floor. His hand jerked a couple of times as if he was still trying to draw his gun but then stopped, and as the last breath of air rushed from his body, he relaxed and his lifetime of terror came to an end.

Lane came running through the door with his pistol up, but when he saw the outlaw lying dead on the floor he came to a sliding stop. Then looking at Becky he asked, "you ok?"

She gave him a nod, then holstering the still smoking six-gun, she ran into Lane's arms. And as their lips softly met she whispered, "I love you, Lane Tipton, and I'm so glad you're home."

"Hey, Sheriff," Tater said, "is this the gal you're thinking about marryin'?"

"Not thinking about it, Tater. This is the one I'm going to marry."

"All I can say is, you better stay on her good side or work on your draw because I can tell you right now you ain't fast enough."

"I know, I grew up with her. She's always been faster

than me," Lane admitted with a smile, "and faster than most of the men in these parts."

Once again gunfire echoed through the night from the direction of the schoolhouse and when it had faded, Blackie Getts and all the members of his gang were dead.

The towns folk walked from the hotel, rejoicing at the news that all of the outlaws had been killed and the sight of Blackie Getts lying dead on the floor of the Double Deuce brought a warm smile to the aged faces of both Mrs. Scott and Mrs. McNare.

By morning the storm had moved on east, and by midday the Van Dill brothers had arrived with several more men from the Running T.

Two days later, the water had subsided and the day after that, the town of Deer Creek started burying their dead.

They also buried the six outlaws, but not in the town's cemetery and to their graves they added no markers. And it came as no surprise to anyone when Lane asked Tater to stay on as his deputy.

Now with all the horrible death and destruction behind them, the good folks of the little town of Deer Creek could start thinking about things that were more pleasant, like getting ready for two big weddings, the one they had already been planning for Lane and Becky and a second for Sam and Mrs. Mahony.